To Keith

Introduction

Green Days by the River is Michael Anthony's third novel. All three have dealt with the world of the child, and have shown the West Indian reality as it appears to the mind being formed by it. Of course, other West Indian novelists have used child narrators, notably Geoffrey Drayton in *Christopher* and George Lamming in *In the Castle of my Skin*. But none has remained more scrupulously than Anthony within the limits of consciousness imposed by the selection of a child as the guiding intelligence of the work. Perhaps the closest rivals are Andrew Salkey's children's stories, which show a real feel for the minds of children, but even in these, directed towards children as they are, we feel the author's hand as an occasionally intrusive force. By comparison with these writers Anthony is a purist, and he has suffered the consequences. The early critical response, especially in the Caribbean itself, was confused and angry at the apparent aimlessness of the novels. When *Green Days by the River* appeared the reviewer for the Jamaican newspaper *The Sunday Gleaner* commented:

> Just as was said of *The Year in San Fernando*, the author is extremely accurate in portrayal of each incident so that each and every one sounds authentic so that one is forced to ask the question 'so what?' or 'was the story worth telling?'

In Anthony's novel there is no direct authorial intervention between the consciousness of the child narrator and the adult reader. As a result the reader may feel lost, unable to discover his perspectives in the world which the novel describes. But in compensation he is engaged with that world more intensely and more immediately than he could hope to be in a novel where his judgements are more consciously controlled and where his exposure to the actual confused process of experience is less total and less open.

Green Days by the River traces the response of its teenage hero (fifteen-year-old Shell) to the transitional world between childhood and maturity. Like Anthony's earlier narrator, the twelve-year-old Francis of *The Year in San Fernando*, Shell is adjusting to a new and strange environment. Because of his father's illness, which prevents him from holding down a steady job, the family have moved from the beach to Pierre Hill, an inland village on the fringes of the 'bush'. Shell is 'a new feller up here. From Radix'. The new world he encounters is a paradigm for the larger new world of adulthood against which he tests the values of his now fading childhood and the potency of his maturing emotions. During the period of just under a year which the novel covers, we see Shell facing the multiple, overlapping crises of adolescence. His father is dying, and Shell is faced with the inevitable loss of the parent to whom he has always felt closest. He is faced too with a growing awareness of himself as a sexual being, and is at a loss to discover a proper correlation between his feelings, the responses of 'girls' and the demands which the adult world makes on him as a result of these new emotions. In addition, the illness of his father and his subsequent loss as an example and guide to Shell, forces him to seek out new masculine patterns on which to model his behaviour in the adult world to which he now has to adjust.

Green Days by the River is a more complex and ambitious book than *The Year in San Fernando*. Like Anthony's first book, *The Games Were Coming*, it seeks to present a wider range of characters, events, and places – but it retains the technique of *The Year in San Fernando* with its single, shaping intelligence and isolated viewpoint. The principal difference between Francis and Shell as narrators is the difference in their ages. Whereas to the twelve-year-old Francis the world he inhabits is a place where he is more acted upon than active, where he has to try to find recurring patterns in the actions of those around him to guide his own responses, the fifteen-year-old Shell is continually called upon to choose courses of action, although he is only marginally further advanced towards understanding the motives which prompt people to kindness or cruelty, action or passivity, love or hate.

The novel deals very sensitively with Shell's relationship with his father. Although it is clear that he and Shell are very close, when the novel opens we are aware of a potential estrangement as Shell obscurely 'blames' his father for being ill and weak. It is this feeling which draws Shell initially to Mr Gidharee, the fierce and masterful Indian crop-planter and owner of the frightening pack of Tobago dogs. Shell's relationship with his father is a touchstone to which we return throughout the novel but initially it is overlaid by this fascination with Gidharee, whose health and energy make him an attractive surrogate father to replace the ailing Mr Lammy.

> From the time we came to Pierre Hill, Pa had worked for a week, and then he fell sick. Somehow I wished he was as big and strong as Mr Gidharee, instead of being always ill in bed. (p. 2)

When Gidharee, feeling sorry for the Lammy family, invites Shell to come and help him work his land on the river bank at Cedar Grove, he seems to Shell a figure of kindness, whose fierceness, though frightening, is admirable. The boy admires the casual way in which he handles the pack of hunting dogs, and tries to emulate him, even to the point of trying throughout the novel to dress like him and so establish himself in Gidharee's eyes as a real man. Soon the reader is made aware that Gidharee has come to see Shell as an ideal successor, a potential son-in-law, and the next cultivator of the land at Cedar Grove. During the course of their visits to the river-bank, the relationship changes to a more frankly educative one, with Gidharee clearly trying to inculcate in the young Shell his own passion for the bush, and for the planting of crops. It also becomes clear that he has thought of Shell as a potential match for his daughter Rosalie. Shell had been attracted to Rosalie, and he is now confused, since he believed she had rejected him in favour of the dynamic Joe. His own highly romantic attachment to Joan, the girl from Sangre Grande whom he had met at the Discovery Day fair after Rosalie's rejection, seems to him to preclude any relationship with her. His confusion is partly the result of his own naïvety and his failure to read accurately the behaviour of those around him, especially Rosalie; but, although he is obscurely aware of this he fails to see how he can now react except by sticking stubbornly to the commitments he feels he has made.

Life was so strange, and girls so hard to understand. At the Discovery Fair I had wanted Rosalie so much and would have done anything to win her, but she had been too busy running after Joe to bother about me. But Joe did not care. Now that I had got me a girl-friend she seemed to be running after me.

Of course there was no wavering in my mind regarding Joan and Rosalie. Since that day in Sangre Grande Joan had become everything to me. Having her, I no longer cared about any other girl.

I had not seen Joe for some time and I had heard he had gone away to learn to be a motor mechanic. I wondered what had developed between Rosalie and himself. The answer was bound to be nothing. I thought maybe Rosalie had realised by now that he did not care. I wondered what made her return to me all of a sudden. I did not mind this very much, but the friendlier she was to me, it was the nicer Mr Gidharee became, and now he was always asking me to go to Cedar Grove with him. He was the sort of person you couldn't help liking very much. Rosalie was nice too, and pretty, and I had several times thought of making the most of her, but somehow I did not want to do this, for Mr Gidharee's sake. Also, I could not think of Joan and flirt with Rosalie. It was impossible. Whenever I thought of it something just went dead inside me. (p. 94)

In passages like this Anthony captures Shell's struggle to establish a set of values which will make sense of the confusing world he has to face and his increasing feeling that he is being trapped by actions and attitudes over which he has had no real control. There is an essential difference here, too, in the distance established between Shell and the reader in such passages, and the distance we associate with an 'unreliable' narrator, i.e. a narrator whose values are clearly differentiated from the author's values as they appear in the overall tone of the book. The distance established here does not operate ironically. Although we are aware that in the course of arriving at the above decision Shell is actually changing his mind about it, we are not meant to see this as evidence of duplicity on his part, nor are we as readers permitted to feel superior to his judgement. The closeness with which we are made to participate in Shell's thought forces us to see that his confusion is a sympton of his desire to find some stable value within himself which will satisfy the conflicting demands which the outside world seems to make on him.

We are never allowed to be quite sure how aware Shell is of the pressures placed on him. In the section where Gidharee makes it clear that he is contemplating a marriage between Shell and Rosalie there is no attempt to delineate Shell's response.

> 'How old you is now Shell?' he said.
>
> 'Fifteen – going on sixteen.'
>
> 'Rosalie's just on fifteen,' he said.
>
> There was a pleased look over his face. At the word 'Rosalie', I had shifted my eyes quickly and looked at the river. There was silence. Then Mr Gidharee bent down to his work again. I watched him and thought quite a bit until the evening came down and he stopped work. (p. 66)

This omission of part of the narrator's consciousness is clearly a device which the novelist can use to force the reader to speculate or to build tension, and Anthony uses it for both these purposes. But more than this, it is indicative of the way in which the narrator *does not know* since he is unable to formulate even to himself the full significance either of the events or his own reactions to them. Oftentimes he seems to sense what is happening, and is shown to be aware of the shifting attitudes of those around him, but he cannot formulate a coherent explanation nor fully understand why his own responses have shaped themselves in the way they have. For example, when Gidharee first offers him a share of the produce they are harvesting at Cedar Grove, Shell is literally at a loss to explain the action, or even his own response to it, though we are allowed to see that he is aware of more subtle levels of motivation than he can articulate, and of possible conflicting interpretations opened up by the action.

Across the river, on the other bank, I could see balata trees. There were some palms like water-carat beneath them, and there were mangoes all along the edge. It was a thick impenetrable sort of bush on the other side, and it looked very creepy and snaky to me.

'You better cut, Shell, because what you cut is yours'. Mr Gidharee's voice made me jump. And then I took in what he said.

'Mine', I said. 'My own?'

'You don't want it?'

'Yes,' I said. 'Pa'd be glad.'

'But sure,' he said, 'you know what it is to be sick all the time and can't get up to do nothing. I mean if he was working that's a different thing.'

I was very touched and I did not know how to take this. For it looked as though Mr Gidharee had come to this place today just for our sakes. I wanted to thank him but I felt embarrassed and I just remained silent. (p. 24)

Shell's 'I did not know how to take this' is the expression of a literal truth. For much of the novel there is no possibility of recording his complete response, because it does not exist in any formulated way. It is this, too, which makes it so difficult for the reader to achieve a fixed sense of character, since Shell's response, which channels all the action, shifts violently from pole to pole as he struggles to understand a world in which, from his viewpoint, actions of kindness and cruelty, of affection and coldness often seem to arise in an arbitrary pattern. So, the passage above is followed immediately by a violent shift of tone when Lion, one of Gidharee's dogs, captures a live iguana which Gidharee beheads with his matchet. In Shell's eyes the action is a sudden and terrifying realisation that Gidharee's strength can be destructive as well as generous. His resulting confusion is communicated directly to the reader who is forced to realise that in this novel he must respond along with the narrator and cannot indulge in a protective distance from which to make his judgements.

> I heard Mr Gidharee saying, as if to himself, 'It looks as if this boy don't like "guana"?' Then he said, 'Lion, boy, when I tell people how you does hunt for me they doesn't believe, you know.' I glanced round to see what was happening and this time I all but fainted. He had taken off the iguana's head with his cutlass and the bleeding iguana was still whipping and struggling to get away. (p. 25)

Sometimes entire episodes are presented only as implied action, presumably because we are to realise that Shell has been unable to organise a coherent response to them, and the intrusion of an authorial voice, able to supply this deficiency, would serve only to destroy his credibility. For example, in the strange little episode with Sonia, the older girl who gathers the picked cocoa-pods and who comes upon Shell taking his after-work bath in the river near the field. After the episode Shell reflects on the similarity between Sonia's natural acceptance of nakedness and sexual differences as a part of everyday existence, and his father's easy attitude which has created the bond of openness between them.

> Soon I was almost dry and I slung the imaginary rope into the bushes. My hair was still wet, though, and I rubbed it with my hands and it made my hands very wet. Somehow I was feeling very wholesome about Sonia now that she had gone. It was almost a shock to find her so natural and easy. She was not unsettled by my nakedness but took it as

a joke. It did not matter to her. She had not come back for me to be daring with her as I had begun to think. She was the second person I had met who was so much like my father. I thought I would tell Joan about it when I wrote to her that night. (p. 107)

This swift transition to Joan, and the reference to Sonia as the 'second person' so to remind him, remain inexplicable until we recall that he had felt the same tolerance and acceptance to characterise Joan's mother's reception of him as her boy-friend on his visit to her home in Sangre Grande (p. 83). The omission of any overt structure of connecting links allows us to become aware of a growing point in Shell's consciousness just as Shell himself becomes aware of it.

Even more striking an example of the use of omission as narrative technique is in the absence of a direct description of Shell's sexual encounter with Rosalie. We learn of it only by implication in his confused attempts afterwards to understand why he has acted as he has, against his express intentions and his father's warnings of the likely consequences.

When I got back into the house it was very late. My mother had already returned and was in bed. I sneaked in and seeing that Pa was not on the little bed I was relieved and I lay down there to sleep. Having slept all day sleep would not come to my eyes now and I kept thinking about Rosalie. I could not get her out of my mind. I lay face down, and my heart was thumping against the mattress. After a while I got up and crept softly to the cupboard and poured myself a huge drink of rum. I was hoping to knock myself out so I could get to sleep and forget. I was terrified as to what could happen. Both Rosalie and myself were stark staring mad. I asked myself why in the name of reason I was so crazy. My father had warned me about this thing. I was wild and furious with myself . . . (p. 143)

This omission and the credibility it establishes for Shell's narration is part of the technique by which Anthony demonstrates to the reader that he is in the presence of genuine experience, not merely conventionalised stereotype. Anthony resists the temptation to formalise the boy's consciousness, and so allows us to exercise our own intuition and understanding. Kenneth Ramchand has called this quality in his writing a sign of the narrator's 'open consciousness' (See *The West Indian Novel and its Background*: Barnes and Noble, New York, 1970, pp. 205–222). It is a quality responsible for the deep involvement which the reader feels with the action, since it forces him to share the contradictory formulating responses of the narrator in an immediate way. It is also, in the best sense of the word, a 'liberal' technique, since it militates against our siding for or against characters in any simple pattern of values. So, at the end of the novel, it is fruitless to speculate on whether Mr Gidharee is presented as a 'good' or a 'bad' character, or whether the author wishes us to 'approve' of his actions or not.

In their introduction to *The Year in San Fernando* (Caribbean Writers Series) Paul Edwards and Kenneth Ramchand rightly stress that: 'Anthony is not interested in an ironic contrast between the boy's innocent vision and the reader's experienced interpretation', although they recognise it as 'part of the novel's technique that the reader should be able to "recognise" some of these experiences over Francis' head'. (op. cit. p. xviii). However, whether as a result of earlier criticism, or because of the needs imposed by a more complex plot and more varied characters, in *Green Days by the River* Anthony has been forced to develop the author's rhetorical control over the reader to a more marked degree. Although such controls are obviously part of the technique of *The Year in San Fernando* too, they are here developed with more insistence and in more obvious forms. Perhaps the most notable example of these 'signposts' to the reader's response is the skein of hunting and trapping images associated with Mr Gidharee throughout the novel. Images which prepare us, in a way the narrator is unable to do directly, for Shell's sense at the end of the novel that somehow he has unwittingly lost his 'freedom', and that for better or for worse Mr Gidharee has 'caught' him. The imagery forces itself on the reader's attention, so that he is able to dismiss it as a rhetorical control only with a wilful effort. For example in chapter 18: when the chapter opens Shell seems to have achieved his ambition and, with the exception of his short pants, has dressed himself as a complete replica of Mr Gidharee. On their way to Cedar Grove, Tiger, one of the dogs, has a brush with a pig, an episode which prepares us for the possibility that Gidharee's dogs, under his orders, may be induced to hunt more than deer and iguana, as indeed they do in chapter 26 when they attack Shell. In the conversation which follows Shell seems to realise that Gidharee is taking a remarkably keen interest in the progress of his relations with Rosalie. The sapodillas which Gidharee gives Shell as part of his 'share' of the Cedar Grove produce are described as 'sweet as syrup', and they set off in Shell's mind a train of thought which shows us that subconsciously he is becoming aware of Gidharee's interest as a 'lure', and aware too that there may be a price to be paid later for Gidharee's generosity and kindness.

Mr Gidharee got up and went over to the sack of seeds and plant-slips, looking at the seeds especially, and as I sat there eating sapodillas, I was listening to the birds outside.

There were not so many of them now as when the fruit was in full swing, and now, above us, there was not wild screeching, but the clear and distinct whistling of the songster birds. I was listening particularly to a semp. It was singing rather than twittering. Every note came clear and pure, and as I sat there listening, my thoughts went back to those times when I used to catch birds, and I began remembering how I used to make my cages from *bois-canoe* stalks, and how I used to bleed *lagley* gums from breadfruit trees, and set the stickiest *lagley* all round the top of my cage, and perch my cage, with my best semp inside, right on the top of a pole, in the bushes, and how I would hide myself away, listening to my semp calling the other birds. As soon as a bird was lured to rest on the cage, and got itself stuck on the *lagley* I would pounce out from my hiding place. (p. 117)

If we miss the similarity of the fable and the situation with Gidharee as snarer, Rosalie as bait, and Shell as victim, Anthony follows it up with an unmistakable directing image, even less exclusively rooted in Shell's consciousness, though not actively intrusive to it, when he implies a comparison between the two stages of the bird's life, represented by the *jeune male* (young male) and the *vieux male* (old male) and the two stages of human life represented by Shell and Gidharee.

I was wondering why was it we gave our Trinidad birds French names like *jeune male* and *vieux male*. The *vieux male* was very beautiful with yellow under its belly and blue on its back and wings. It was very beautiful but it had already lost its singing voice. But when it was young, it sung fine. That's to attract the female, I thought. The girls. But even then it could not touch the semp, for notes. I did not think I would keep birds any more though. I was too old for that. (p. 120)

It is worth remembering, perhaps, that all novels develop some form of rhetoric and the apparent omission of the author should not be confused with his literal absence as the ultimate arbiter of the action of the book. Nor should we confuse the restraint of style with a lack of control, nor a generosity of conception with an absence of values.

There is a more marked development in Shell than in Francis, though here too it would be wrong to read the story as a sort of 'novel of education'. At the end of the novel he remains confused about many things in his situation; confused, too, about how he has arrived at his present condition; about his feelings – whether he is happy or sad at the outcome of events – and he remains conscious of being unable properly to express much of his feelings.

> Outside the places were very shadowy in the early dawn and this made me feel even more desolate. Fears for my father kept crowding in upon me. And with them, memories of other days came to mind.
>
> All the fine things we had done together – Pa and I – even distant things from Down-the-Beach days were with me now. Even the little things at Pierre Hill, such as sitting beside him on the settee and his putting his arm about my neck and being my chum as well as my father; all the numberless things which I could think of and feel so sharply without being able to tell of.
>
> And yet, if this was goodbye to happy days, perhaps I should be grateful for having Mr Gidharee. Perhaps, grateful even for the dogs. *For I'd never be in want again.* (pp. 194–5)

Once again the crucial event which sets the seal on Shell's fate, the death of his father, is described only implicitly . . .

> After I had phoned the Colonial hospital from there, as Mr Gidharee had asked me to do, as a precaution, I had to hasten to send him a telegram so he could start making arrangements for the funeral (p. 196)

At the end of the novel we are aware that judging the actions of Shell or of Mr Gidharee is irrelevant. If we approach the novel in this way we would be at a loss to explain the renewed affection for Gidharee which Shell never shows in any other way than as some kind of moral 'capitulation' on his part. However, if we try to see it as part of the whole pattern of responses which Gidharee has stirred up in Shell throughout the novel, we see that Shell's confused response here as elsewhere bypasses judgement since it presents confusion as a condition of existence – not a failure of perception or a moral weakness.

In coming to terms with Gidharee, Shell is coming to terms with the human condition as it is, with all its simultaneous and contradictory capacities for good and evil, for compassion and brutality. When, at the end of the novel, Shell remarks that he feels Gidharee's generosity over the funeral has brought him 'nearly as close to him as I had felt to my father' there is no irony intended. It is symptomatic of the realisation, slowly forming in Shell, though not explicit yet, that Gidharee's actions and expectations have been no more nor less 'human' than anyone else's; and that Gidharee's 'brutality' has been provoked by his own confused and inadequate response as much as by anything else. Shell's behaviour at the end of the novel suggests that, for better or for worse, he has taken the first real step out of the world of childhood. Because of this the potentially tragic implications of his losses, both of his father and of his 'choice' disappear, and we are left with Shell facing a reality neither avoidable nor disagreeable, except in the sense that all human conditions are disagreeable and limiting. It is left to the ubiquitous Mr Gidharee to reassure him at the end, and to comfort him through the ugly transition into the real world.

> '. . . Don't worry, everything will be okay.'
> 'I know,' I said.
> 'Everything will be okay, me old Shell,' he said. (p. 198)

Gareth Griffiths
Senior Lecturer in English
University of East Anglia, Norwich, 1973

1

I heard the dogs barking and I knew that old man Gidharee was coming up the road. I went out into the road and there he was, pulling his four dogs behind him and trying to ward off the neighbour's dogs that rushed out after them. There was much barking and it seemed to make an awful racket in the place. Mr Gidharee's dogs were very big Tobago dogs and I knew he had only to let one of them loose to have the others scurrying in again. He was having difficulty in pulling the dogs along, for the cutlass-case at his side kept getting in the way. Then, too, he had a sack strung across his shoulder, and he was also carrying a cocoa-rod.

I had watched him every morning and he had greeted me as he passed. He did not know me well as we had just moved to Pierre Hill. But he had seen how I had admired his big Tobago dogs, and he seemed very friendly towards me.

As he approached now I began to help drive away the other dogs.

'These *blasted* pot-hounds!' he said.

I laughed.

'Every morning,' he said, 'every morning it's the same damn thing!'

We managed to get the strays away and now I was walking along behind him and I patted the black-and-white dog. I had just come to Pierre Hill but Rover knew me already. He wagged his tail. I did not go too near to the others, but they too had seen a lot of me and I was not very much afraid of them. I knew the brown dog was Lion, and the other two were

Hitler and Tiger, but of these two I did not know which was which.

Mr Gidharee went along with the dogs and every time he looked round he seemed surprised I was still there. Now he turned round again and he said, 'You going far from home, boy.'

'It's all right, Mr Gidharee.'

'How you know my name?'

'Don't know,' I had not even thought about that.

He laughed.

I looked at the dogs now, and I said, 'Which one is Tiger and which one is Hitler?'

'This is Tiger.' He pointed to the spotted dog. 'And this one here is Hitler.'

'Oh.'

'I ain't seeing you old man these days.'

'He's sick.'

'Sick? With what?'

'Something like water under the heart.'

He did not seem to have heard of that before. He inclined his head to one side, then the other, and he seemed to be working it out.

I did not even know that Mr Gidharee knew my father. I supposed he just thought it natural I would have a father. I doubted whether he had ever seen him. From the time we came to Pierre Hill, Pa had worked for a week, and then he fell sick. Somehow I wished he was as big and strong as Mr Gidharee, instead of being always ill in bed.

'You know Pa, Mr Gidharee?'

'Ain't he the man who Rosalie showed the place – up here?'

'You mean the *dougla* girl?'

'That's my Ro,' he said, laughing, 'the *dougla* girl.'

He seemed to be amused by my saying 'dougla', which was

the slang everyone used for people who were half Indian and half Negro. As I watched him laughing I thought of her again and of the time my father had asked her the way. I remembered her own laughing eyes and curly hair which was very different from Mr Gidharee's Indian face and Indian hair. He looked at me again and he said, 'Her mother is *creole*, just like you.'

'Yes, I know.' I had already thought that out.

We had by now reached the top of Pierre Hill and the road was beginning to take the downward turn.

'You father not working?' he asked.

'He's sick.'

'Yes, but I mean – in bed?'

'Yes. He have asthma too.'

'Good God!' Then he said, 'Well tell your ma if she could let you come with me one of these mornings.'

'Where?'

'In the bush. On my piece of land. A little garden thing, like. Cedar Grove.'

I did not know where that was.

He pointed ahead. 'Just over the hill, by the Spring Bridge.'

'I'll ask her.'

'Okay.'

I patted Rover, the black-and-white dog, and turned to walk back down the hill. In the distance were the tops of the coconut palms of Plaisance, and above them, the sea. The sun was big and silvery and I had to put my hand over my eyes, for the glare. I did not even know that this girl my father had asked the way lived on Pierre Hill. My father had seen her when he had gone into the cafe. She seemed to be about my age and I had even thought then how pretty she was. I could not remember seeing Mr Gidharee then. I just remembered the girl with her hair in curls. Thinking of her now, she was very vivid in my mind.

My mother had already gone down to Plaisance, by the sea, where she worked in one of the beach-houses. It was hardly any good asking my father about going to Mr Gidharee's little place because if he said yes and my mother said no, it was no. I went into the house and there he was, lying on the little bed. This low, little bed was in a corner of the sitting room, and here was where he slept. He was awake now, and he was breathing rather hard with the asthma.

'Where you was?' he said, 'I was calling you.'

'I was out in the road with Mr Gidharee.'

'Mr who?'

'Mr Gidharee. The man with those big Tobago dogs.'

'You just come up here but you know everybody already.'

'He asked me about you.'

'About me?' He turned round on his side.

'He just asked me if you wasn't working.'

'He have a job for me or what?'

'No, he only ask that. Just so. He want me to go down to his place – you know, a little plantation, like.'

'For what?'

'Don't know.'

'And where's this place?'

'Cedar Grove Road.' I knew he didn't know where that was.

'You better ask your mother,' he said.

I looked at him lying there on the bed and the *dougla* girl sprang to mind.

'Pa, you remember that *dougla* girl down in the cafe who showed you up the hill?'

He thought a little and said, 'Aha.'

'That is her father.'

'You mean the Indian man – Gidharee?'

'Yes. Her mother is *creole*.'

'Oh, I see.'

4

'He laughed when I called her *dougla*.'

'Why? What else you could call her if she's Indian-Creole? It ain't no insult.'

'You don't mean Indian-*Creole* you mean Indian-Negro.' I was baiting him now. We had argued on this word *creole*.

'Okay, Indian-Negro, then,' he said.

'Because *creole* is – '

'Okay, *creole* is the foreign settlers, as those silly teachers tell you in school. Anyway that girl is a *dougla*.'

His eyes avoided me for a moment because he knew I had won my point. Then he looked at me stealthily and we both laughed.

Afterwards I went on thinking about the girl again. If she lived so close to me maybe we'd begin talking somehow. I wondered if she was older than me.

My father saw me sitting quietly so he turned again and said, 'So I suppose you want to go down to the beach to ask your mother?'

'Yes, Pa.'

'Bring that pipe for me before you go. You'll find some tobacco by that jug.'

I did not move. I did not want to give him the pipe. He never smoked when my mother was here but as soon as she went out he would say, 'Bring that pipe for me.' The ridiculous thing was, he kept on hiding his tobacco from Ma, and tobacco was the worst thing to hide. The place reeked of it. He knew he was not supposed to smoke but he *would* keep on. And his asthma was worse than ever this morning.

'Bring the pipe, Shell.'

'Ma say you mustn't smoke.'

'Oh, is that so!'

'Yes.'

He just shrugged and turned his face towards the wall.

I stood looking at him. From as far back as I could remember he had been ill – not throughout, but from time to time – and it was as though he was an invalid. And yet sometimes he would recover from the asthma and would be like any other man, and my mother would say he was as strong as a bull. She was always overjoyed to see him up. But he was never up for long.

I said, 'Well, I going down to Plaisance now. Okay?'

'So you not bringing the pipe?'

'No.'

'All right, well don't stop whole day down Plaisance.'

'Okay.'

'And don't look for the *dougla*.'

I laughed. This took me by surprise. I was only just past fifteen but he always said this sort of thing to me. It was funny how he seemed to know things. As soon as I liked somebody, he knew.

There was a big cashew tree on Pierre Hill and it was in fruit. As I walked out of our yard I picked up a few stones to see if I could pelt down a cashew. When I got into the road and looked towards the cashew tree I saw some boys under it pelting. I went down to the tree and looked for a nice ripe cashew, and I began to pelt at it.

Three boys were there and they were all pelting and talking. The ground was littered with rotting cashews. Sometimes when one of the boys pelted and picked a cashew and the cashew fell and burst, the boy would just pick it up and dust it and eat it.

I was aiming at a nice ripe cashew but it was high and would be very hard to pick. I kept on pelting. The other boys were ploughing stones and sticks up into the tree, but the result was only falling leaves. Then one exclaimed, 'Christ! Look I hit that brute and he wouldn't fall. Come and see – he still shaking! God, that was a shot.'

I laughed. The other boys went round to see the cashew still shaking. I walked round to the other side of the tree and there was the cashew, still quivering from the blow. I was amazed at this, and forgetting that I did not even know the boys, I said, 'That's because it still green.'

'That's a ripe cashew,' the pelter said, 'Jesus Christ! you can't see that cashew ripe?'

It was very high and it was hard to see if it was ripe. This was the red kind of cashew and even when they were young they were red. 'It look green to me,' I said.

'Len, hear this man!' the pelter said. 'He looking at that *rosy* cashew and calling that green!'

The one called Len came and looked again. He said, 'That's a nice ripe, sweet darling But it hard. Like your girl-friend. Nice and sweet but no easy picking.'

I started laughing. Len, seeing I was so amused, came up to me and said, 'This man have a nice little jane, boy, *dougla* and thing, and living just over there, and she always talking to him and laughing and all, man, but he scared to tell her he like her.'

The others were choking with laughter. The pelter pretended that he was not listening and he kept on stoning the high cashew. Then after a little while he dropped the stones he had in his hands and said, 'That bastard too hard.'

'Like Rosalie,' Len said.

'Like your – ' And the pelter checked himself.

'Say it,' Len said, walking up to him, his fist clenched. 'Say it, and I'll make you swallow it.'

The pelter just grinned and walked back a few steps. Len was bigger than him, and looked the toughest of the three. The other fellow was disappointed it did not turn out into a fight. Somehow Len did not even seem cross. I felt they were just having fun together.

Now all three of them sat down on the bank under the cashew tree. There was a drain just before the cashew tree and they sat with their feet in the drain. The pelter said, 'If I only get vex I'll climb and pick that bugger.'

The one who had not said anything yet said, 'I don't really want no cashew. This cashew too rack. I only feel like pelting, that's all.'

I said to Len, 'Rack? What's that?'

'Oh, what we call "rack" is when this sorta funny juice sorta tie up your tongue, you know. Make your mouth feel sticky and funny.'

'Oh, I know.'

Len turned to the pelter again. 'So how your little jane? Let's talk about your little thing, man.'

The other one said, 'Yes come on, Joe.'

I was walking round the tree, pretending I was looking for good cashews to pelt at, but I was listening to them.

Len said, 'So how's little Rosie – how things going, good?'

I drew nearer. From the time the talk went on Rosalie my heart began racing.

Joe pretended he did not know what they were talking about, and the one called Len looked at me and shook his head. He said, 'Boy, this man! Some people have all the luck!'

'Who is this girl?' I asked.

'She living just over there,' he pointed to the house almost opposite. 'A first-class little *dougla* jane.'

The one who had spoken very little, said, 'He's a new feller, he wouldn't know.'

Len snapped, 'Why you don't shut-up shop! He know more about Pierre Hill than you.' Then he turned to me, 'You don't know that little sugar-plum, boy – the mother is *creole*, and father, Indian?'

'With big Tobago dogs?' I said.

'See what I mean?' Len cried. 'You saying he don't know nothing. He know more about them than you.'

8

The quiet fellow looked shame-faced; Joe, the pelter, seemed very surprised that I had already known this.

I said, 'So that's your girl-friend, Joe?'

'My girl-friend? This Lennard is a joker, boy.'

'Oh, come on, Joe,' Lennard said, 'you know she have a soft spot for you.'

Joe looked at me rather shyly. 'Don't bother with them,' he said.

I was looking at the ground now, thinking of Rosalie and remembering that face again. Then I said, 'She's nice.'

The one who had looked quiet said, 'Joe, you'll have to watch out for this man.'

Lennard turned round at him, 'Why you don't shut your trap! Why you don't leave the feller alone!'

They had all forgotten about pelting cashew now and the talk was all Rosalie. I listened to them for a while longer and then I said, 'See you fellers. Have to go down to the beach.'

'Going already?' Lennard said.

'Yes, have to go now.'

'Okay, then,' he said. The pelter looked round and said, 'Okay, then.' The other one said, 'See you.'

I could not help thinking about Rosalie as I went on – and about the three boys, especially the pelter. We were all about the same age, around fifteen. Lennard was the most friendly to me but somehow he seemed a bully. The pelter looked quite easy-going, and he was nice-looking, and I could imagine Rosalie liking him. He was only excited when he was pelting the cashew. The other fellow had spoken the least of all and I did not even know his name. I was glad, though, to have made friends with them. They were my first friends of Pierre Hill.

It was close on a fortnight since I had seen that *dougla* girl and yet I could not get her out of my head. In fact, having just heard the boys talk about her she was more than ever in my mind now. I wondered whether she really liked Joe, or whether those two fellows were only having a game with him. I wondered if she was a friendly girl or if she would be hard to get to talk to. And then I thought of Mr Gidharee and how he and I were growing to be friends. I would certainly like to go to Cedar Grove with him now, wherever it was! I put on some speed in my walking and in little time I was on the beach.

2

The next miorning when I heard the tumult of the dogs I came out into the road to tell Mr Gidharee Ma had said yes.

'Right,' he said, 'well – you'll be ready for tomorrow morning?'

'Yes.'

'You see I only going to plant today. But tomorrow morning, come, and bring a bag – a big bag – and we staying whole day.'

'Okay.'

He walked up the hill, the dogs on leashes, following, their mouths open and their tongues hanging out, red, their eyes looking anxious and keen. I went back home and looked for a large bag and I kept it ready. Then I went down to the cashew tree but none of the boys were there this morning. I pelted at the same cashew I had been pelting at on the previous morning, and having no success, I started to pelt at the one Joe had hit. With the second shot I cut the stem cleanly with a flying stone and the cashew came tumbling through the leaves. I could not get under it to catch it, through being blinded by the leaves, and

10

it fell *bash!* on the ground and burst. It was no good, then. It just made a mess under the tree.

I stood over it looking at it, feeling awful, and yet feeling excited. If when I met the boys I told them that I'd picked this rosy cashew, cutting the stem cleanly in two tries, they would not believe. I would swear to God that I did but they would never believe. Only they would see it was not on the tree any more.

I wished someone had been there to see me make that shot! I thought of it as a shot in a life-time. I had not even stopped to aim properly. It was like magic! Still, it achieved nothing, for the cashew lay bashed on the ground.

This depressed me now. I stooped over the fruit and wrung off the nut on top, and at once the idea came to me – why not wring off all the nuts of the fallen cashews and take them home and roast them and make *cashew-nuts*? I went round wringing off the nuts and suddenly I jumped, as two hands clamped down over my eyes.

After a few seconds of panic and struggling I managed to remove the hands and turning round, it was Lennard. I was panting but amused from the surprise. 'I didn't see when you come up,' I said. My heart was pounding like a drum.

He was convulsed in laughter. As I gathered up the nuts he had made me spill, I noticed him glancing to the house across the road.

Then he said! 'You does eat cashew or *cashew*-nuts!'

'I like roast cashew-nuts. You?'

'I don't like cashew anyhow,' he said.

I went on wringing off the nuts. Then I sprang up. 'Look, Len, you know I pick that high cashew – the one Joe hit yesterday!'

'Eh?'

11

'I picked that rosy cashew Joe hit. Second chance! Oh God, boy, that was a shot!'

He merely gave a half-smile, his head still turned towards the Gidharee's house. He said nothing. This shocked and hurt me. I had expected he would argue about it. I had been sure he would doubt and deny it. I looked up at him but he was still gazing across the road.

A few moments passed, with me being very sour, and afterwards I looked down again and I said, 'Where's Joe?'

'Don't know. If anything he'll soon be up here. He wouldn't leave the little *dougla* in peace.'

'But you said she was his jane.'

'We was only making him feel nice.'

While talking he was glancing at the Gidharee's house every now and again and I was beginning to have my own suspicions. He said, 'That little thing doesn't go out at all. They must be saving her up or something!'

'Who is her boy-friend?'

'Don't know. Don't think she have any boy-friend.'

'I mean, she really nice. I only see her once though.'

'That is the sweetest thing in the *whole* of Mayaro,' Lennard said. Then he said, 'I don't know but I like *dougla* people bad. I really wouldn't mind, boy.'

I laughed. Yesterday, the way he had spoken I had not the slightest idea that he was interested in Rosalie. This was a surprise to me now.

'How old you think she is?' I said.

'About fourteen so.'

'That look like robbing the cradle,' I said, as a joke.

'Robbing the cradle? That's only a year younger than me. Don't know about you but I really wouldn't mind. I like *dougla* people bad, boy.'

He kept staring at the Gidharees' house. There was a hibiscus hedge in front of the house and there was not much to be seen from where we were. The gateway was a little further down. After a while Lennard said, 'You know, this does get me! That blasted little jane doesn't go out *at all*!'

'Don't worry,' I said, 'let's pelt cashew.'

3

Bright and early the next morning I got up and waited for Mr Gidharee. Knowing now that he was the father of the *dougla* girl, and having spoken so much about her, I felt a little in awe of him. But on the whole I liked him. My mother had already left with the first light, and my father was lying on the little bed, rather worse than usual. Seeing me stirring, he remembered I was going with Mr Gidharee to Cedar Grove and he said, 'When you coming back?'

'This evening. Ma said it's all right. She left everything where you could get it.'

'But you and this Gidharee well *thick*,' he said. 'Why?'

'Don't know.'

I started laughing. I knew he meant this had to do with the *dougla* girl. He turned his head and he saw I understood and he laughed.

I said, 'You'll be all right? Until I come back?'

'Think so. Pass the pipe for me.'

'No.'

'Okay go on. Don't frighten for me.'

'Okay, then, see you.' I went out into the yard.

Soon there came the riot of barking and I went for the bag

13

and folded it and I took a cutlass. This cutlass was not like Mr Gidharee's, but an ordinary house cutlass. It had no long, curving handle, and narrow, sword-like blade. I would have given a great deal to hold one like that this morning, and to have had a case, like Mr Gidharee's, hanging from my belt.

I hurried out into the road. Mr Gidharee was standing there with the dogs. 'Right,' he said, 'that's the man.'

I was wearing my thick blue-dock pants and khaki shirt and on my feet I had my father's old sandals, for the prickles. I felt like a real working man. Mr Gidharee looked at me approvingly.

'That's it. We'll work like hell today.'

I felt good.

'Look, you take Rover,' he said, 'he know you.'

He passed Rover's lead to me. The barking of the loose dogs had got Rover excited and as I took the lead he rushed forward, jerking me along. 'Rover!' Mr Gidharee shouted at him. The dog stopped and looked back. Mr Gidharee said to me, 'He too strong for you.'

'Is all right. I'll hold him.'

'It's these good-for-nothing little so-and-so's, you know!' He looked round, furious, at the dogs that came from the yards of the other roadside houses. A few of the dogs were strays and did not belong anywhere in particular. Long after we had moved off some of them stood up in the road, watching. This amused me in a way because it looked as though they enjoyed the tumult. We went along, Rover still tugging me forward every now and again.

These four dogs were so huge that each one of them was nearly as high as my waist. When they barked the echoes seemed to rebound from the forest. They were all panting now, from the heat, their mouths open, their tongues hanging out. Rover seemed the healthiest and handsomest and I was glad to be holding him. He was so powerful, it seemed more sensible to ride him than to walk behind him. I was only hoping he would not lunge forward suddenly and drag me along.

I was walking a little behind Mr Gidharee to keep out of the middle of the road. Rover was walking on the roadside grass, and I noticed that the other three were doing the same. It was because the pitch was getting hot. Tiger, the spotted dog, was very frisky and was crossing and intertwining with the other two, causing Mr Gidharee to be constantly unravelling the leads. Hitler and Lion were fairly calm. They trotted with swinging tails and they put their noses to every crack or crevice in the ground.

'How you going, all right?' Mr Gidharee called, looking back for me. We were on the top of the hill now and there was the long winding road to go down.

'Yes.'

'You know Cedar Grove?'

'I think I know where it is but I never went down there.'

'Oho.'

'But I know Spring Flat.'

'Oh, well from there it ain't far. When you get to Spring Flat and you could see the bridge, well it's just on the side of the bridge.'

'Oh.'

I watched him walking there before me, his broad leathern belt jerking in rhythm with his hips. He was walking in the 'one-for-today, one-for-tomorrow' style, and he did not seem to be going fast but I had to make an effort to keep up with him. Rover was used to his pace and following him, and whenever I was tending to slow down the lead tugged me forward.

'Don't worry,' Mr Gidharee called again, 'it ain't far now.'

Having long passed the houses of Pierre Hill, we were now almost on Spring Flat. Here, it was mostly bush on either side of the road, and as we began to enter the Flat, there were springs in the bushes. I watched Mr Gidharee's back view and how his greying hair fell onto the back of his neck. His shoulders were broad and square, and his back had a flatness from his shoulders right down – as if he had no behind at all. The dogs, getting the smell of the forests, were more frisky now, and more difficult to manage. Mr Gidharee looked round to see how I was getting on.

'You having trouble with him?'

'No.'

'What's your name? I mean I don't even know what they call you.'

'Shellie.'

'Oh, "Shellie". Okay, Shell, we ain't have far now, boy.'

Spring Flat was cool and shady from the tall immortelle trees. There were a lot of cocoa trees between the immortelles and you could smell the tang of cocoa in the air. The road was straight for a good way before us, and rising in the distance were the two tall girders of the Spring Bridge.

Just before the bridge I could see a red road running away to the left, and this was Cedar Grove. Reaching it, we turned along it, and at once we were in a strange world of forests and shade and strongly-scented flowers and fruit, and in a world of bird-song, and of dry leaves almost covering the red macadam road. Mr Gidharee stopped and freed the dogs and they frisked and ran barking up the road.

Soon we turned off Cedar Grove itself into a little track, and the dogs had already bolted up this track and had disappeared.

Mr Gidharee drew his cutlass from the case and nudged me: 'Always keep you cutlass in your hand when you in the bush. You never know.'

I unwrapped my cutlass from the sugar-bag and held it in my hand. We were now surrounded by giant trees and thick undergrowth, and there was ceaseless chirping and singing from the birds in the trees. Every now and again one of the dogs startled me by suddenly springing out of the undergrowth, and occasionally there would be a yelp from one of them, way ahead.

'You all right, Shell?' Mr Gidharee called over his shoulder.

'Yes.'

We were walking single file in this narrow track and every few moments he looked round for me.

'You walking like cat on hot ashes. I could see you ain't accustomed to the bush.' He laughed.

'I accustom to bush all right.'

'Don't give me that. You from Down-the-beach. Down-the-beach people don't know about bush.'

I laughed quietly behind him, watching my step, picking my way.

'Look the place just over there,' he said. 'You see those boundary flowers? From there back.'

Now I could see the red boundary flowers, where the forest suddenly cleared, and beyond that I could see the bank and the yellow-brown Ortoire, flowing by. In a few moments we reached the boundary flowers, and from there to the river was a vast field of rice.

There was a path along the side of the rice-field and we followed it. 'We'll come back here in the rice later,' Mr Gidharee said. 'Let's go on the other side.' He put two fingers to his mouth and whistled and one of the dogs came dashing out of the forest and plunged straight into the rice-field.

'God blast you!' Mr Gidharee cried. 'Get out of the dam' rice.'

The dog hurried out of the rice-field wagging its tail.

'And it's Tiger again,' he said, fuming at the dog. 'The son-of-a-who-cut-your-head! You is the oldest bugger, you know – *you* should know better!'

By now the other three dogs had come, and Rover, the black-and-white one, was just beside me, wagging his tail, his mouth open, tongue out, blowing. I patted him.

Mr Gidharee looked from the crushed part of the field to Tiger, and from Tiger to the crushed part of the field. Then he turned to me: 'Never see any bleddy thing like this! Anyway dam' good thing this rice good to cut orready. Else I'd – ' He stood there biting his lips with anger. Then he shook his head and we started walking again.

Lion, the brown dog, led the way. Tiger, already recovered, was standing up, looking into the bushes, its ears pricked. I looked back for the other two. Rover had disappeared again, but I saw Hitler, the black one, hind leg against a tree, passing water.

As we walked on Mr Gidharee said, 'Shell, boy, you mustn't mind me. I does curse bad. Can't help it. That's all my fault; curse bad, and a little drink – that's all.' He smiled nicely, as if to say he was a nice man otherwise.

I smiled back to show approval. He said, 'But these dogs would make an angel curse his mother. You know I did really feel to *plan-ass* that Tiger!' He passed his hand on the flat side of his blade as though he regretted not having used it. Then he said, wistfully, 'And yet the thing is – the thing is, I don't know what I'd do without these dogs.'

'No,' I said.

Rover jumped out of the bush into the path and startled me. Mr Gidharee mumbled on: 'How I could ever do without them! I could ever do without them? Never. You know how much money I spend on these so-and-so dogs every day?'

The rice-field ended and the section we walked into now was full of fruit trees. The smell of oranges came strongly to me, and there was also the smell of sapodillas, and I began looking around at the leaves, and started sniffing, because I was sure there was also star-apple – which we called kymeat. Now there was little growth under the trees and the grass was cut low, so you could walk anywhere. There was a little wooden hut ahead and a track leading up to it. When we got to the hut Mr Gidharee stuck his cutlass into the ground, and the blade sung, and he unstrung his knapsack from his shoulder.

He said, 'You like orange?'

'Oh yes.'

'Well I think we better suck a few orange, eh, before we do anything. First things first.'

I stuck my cutlass into the ground. Above, the place was yellow with ripe oranges, and there was a tangerine tree nearby – and still the faint smell of star-apple was coming to me.

'You ain't have no brothers and sisters?'

'No, just me alone.'

'Pity,' he said. 'If nobody ain't eat up these fruits the birds will just gobble them down just like that. Look at those corn-birds in that blasted tree!'

I looked up at the tree and I, too, grew annoyed. Something should be done about this sort of thing. It was plain he could not sell this fruit. Nobody could sell fruit in Mayaro. Who would buy fruit when there was so much to steal? I had never seen so many fruit trees in my life. The branches overhead were full of fruit, and there were fruit trees stretching away beside us and in front up to the river. Yet sapodillas cost a fortune in Port-of-Spain – according to Pa, anyway – and people were glad to get them. Mr Gidharee saw my face and perhaps he knew I was disheartened.

'Don't worry,' he said, 'you mustn't worry about that kinda thing. Let's suck a few oranges and console weself.'

There was a cocoa-rod leaning up against the hut and he took it and went to one of the orange trees.

'No, I'll climb,' I said. I did not want the oranges to fall on the ground and burst.

'You could climb orange trees? Down-the-beach people can't climb, you know. They could only climb coconut trees.'

This amused me. He was half teasing, half serious. What he said was true, too in a way. There were mainly coconut trees along the sea-front. Lots of people were afraid to climb orange trees, because of the thorns, but orange trees were easy to climb. 'I'll climb it,' I said.

'Go ahead. Okay by me. You could put your things in the shack.'

I was beginning to feel warm and friendly towards him. At first he was just a stranger who had asked me to come to Cedar Grove with him, but now he was a little more than that. I took up the bag from the ground, and I took both cutlasses, and the knapsack, and I carried them to the hut. The door was half-open and when I went in there was Tiger lying in the middle of the hut.

'Oh, Tiger, boy, you here? Nearly made me jump.' I stood looking at him. Then I said, 'No wonder you nearly got *planassed*.'

Tiger made a little whine and wagged his tail. I tried to stroke him. I touched his forehead. He made a slight growl. 'We must get to be friends,' I said. 'Let's be friends. You is a hell of a Tiger – I mean to say, you growling at *me*?' He gave a yawn and scratched his belly with his paws. He was lying flat on his side. I tried to stroke him and yet I was afraid to touch him, and then I was touching him lightly and then I was actually stroking him, and he wasn't making any sound. I felt thrilled. Then after a moment I said, 'Okay – I going to suck some orange, boy.'

I put the things down and outside I went. Mr Gidharee was sitting on the grass under the orange tree. Hitler and Lion were lying in patches of sun a little distance away. The corn-birds and parakeets were chirping wildly, and the smell of fruit strongly scented the air.

'Tiger inside there,' I said.

'Where?'

'In the shack.'

'Oh don't bother with that lazy son-of-a gun!'

I had started to climb the tree but I could hardly climb, for laughing. He was laughing too. 'What you laughing for?' he said. 'You like to hear me curse, boy?'

I was choking with laughter. It was the way he said things that made me laugh so. And it was the way he cursed so fluently. I had to get down again and wait a little before I could start climbing again.

'Ah, boy,' Mr Gidharee said, 'can't help it. That is the only thing with me. Everybody does say so. But I don't mean anything.'

I was soon up among the oranges and was reaching for some nice yellow ones and he got up from the ground to catch. After catching the first one, he cried. 'Wait a minute. I'll tell you if this tree sweet.' He tore the orange in half and put it to his mouth – rind and all – and before he could talk he began shaking his head approvingly. Then he spat out the seeds. 'This orange sweet like honey. Send down. Ah ketching.'

After I had picked enough oranges I began looking around at the place. On one side was the river – big, broad Ortoire – easing along and winding away into jungle forests. On the other side stout trees rose up from the edge of the path, and from here, the red boundary flowers gave the feeling of setting the ground alight.

'You all right? You coming down?'

I looked down. Through a fork in the branch I could see him there below. He had a jack-knife out – one of those big jack-knives with the corkscrew – and I could see he was trying to peel an orange without breaking the skin. After a moment's silence he looked up to see where I was and he saw me looking at him. He jerked his head to throw back the hair.

'You *stick* up there or what!'

I laughed. I moved to and fro to show him I was not stuck. 'I only watching the place,' I said.

Beyond the fruit trees, in the direction in which the river was flowing, I could see cocoa trees. I could tell they were cocoa right away because of the sharper green – almost black-green – of their leaves, and because of the immortelles. You could tell the immortelles were young and could not give much shade yet. It was already June and they were not even flowering.

I looked down through the fork and there he was, squeezing the orange into his mouth, sucking, and spitting out the seeds. It was funny to me, in a way, because my father sucked oranges just like that. I supposed it was the old-time way to do it. Rover and Hitler were now lying beside him.

'Coming down,' I called.

'No – don't come down. *Live* up there!' He was trying to sound as caustic as possible and this only made me laugh. As I turned on the limb, shaking the branches, birds scurried away in all directions.

4

Mr Gidharee let me climb some other fruit trees and we collected some fruit in an old sack he had. I picked sapodillas, shaddocks, and star-apples, and he showed me where the banana trees were. These had huge bunches of ripe bananas and here was where the birds feasted. Most of the bunches were rotting and fly-infested and the bananas themselves were half-eaten by birds.

'You want?' he said.

'No. Don't really feel like it so much. But I smelling pomerac.'

He smiled and looked up. 'You nose good, boy.'

In the tangle of branches above the banana trees were clusters of the red, pear-shaped fruit we called pomerac, and finding the tree now, I climbed and picked a good deal. When I came down again, he said, 'Okay. What you pick is for you – for when you going home.'

'You don't want none?' I wished he would take some, at least.

'Just a couple for Rosie, that's all.'

I took out some nice ones and put them aside then I pulled up one of the vines on the ground and tied the sack-mouth. Then I took the sack into our little hut and I came back and took Rosalie's fruit into the hut. Tiger, the spotted dog, woke up when I went in the second time, and at once he pricked up his ears and was on the alert.

'Tiger!' I said, 'lazy!' I approached him cautiously. Somehow I was still afraid of this one.

He looked up at me with soft eyes. Then he wagged his tail a little. I went out again, and Mr Gidharee said, 'Listen, we going down by the rice now.'

'All right.'

'When you feel peckish, say. We have plenty roti in the bag.' I said nothing.

He looked at me as if doubtful. 'You ain't one of those *creole* who shame to eat roti!'

'Me? No, Mr Gidharee. Not me.'

'Oho,' he said.

We cut rice paddies for about two hours steadily, working in the part of the field near the river. The sun was hot now, and

Ortoire, like a long, slithering snake, eased by beside us. We were using grass-knives, and after Mr Gidharee had shown me what to do, I did not need any more showing and we cut rice man for man. At first he looked to see how I was getting on, but after that he called to me only now and then. We were cutting the rice paddies in 'hands', and Mr Gidharee himself was very quick. As we cut, I heard the dogs barking in the forest. One of the dogs was barking very deep and distinct. Mr Gidharee got up from the cutting and straightened his back. Then from his face I could tell he was listening to the dogs.

'Lion ketch something,' he said.

I rose too. Mr Gidharee turned his head to one side and listened. He put a finger to his mouth to stop me in case I was going to speak. Then he said, 'Hear how he barking? That bugger ketch something!' Then he bent down again to the cutting.

Across the river, on the other bank, I could see balata trees. There were some palms like water-carat beneath them, and there were mangroves all along the edge. It was a thick, impenetrable sort of bush on the other side, and it looked very creepy and snaky to me.

'You better cut, Shell, because what you cut is yours.' Mr Gidharee's voice made me jump. And then I took in what he said.

'Mine?' I said. 'My own?'

'You don't want it?'

'Yes,' I said, 'Pa'd be glad.'

'But sure,' he said, 'you know what it is to be sick all the time and can't get up to do nothing? I mean if he was working that's a different thing.'

I was very touched and I did not know how to take this. For it looked as though Mr Gidharee had come to this place today just for our sakes. I wanted to thank him but I felt embarrassed and I just remained silent.

24

I was cutting the paddy-rice again, and thinking, when suddenly there was a rush from the bush and Lion bounded straight from the forests in front of me. I jumped and gave a cry.

'What happen?' Mr Gidharee said.

'Look what Lion have in his mouth.'

'Lion, come. Come,' Mr Gidharee said, and he whistled, 'Phee-o! Phee-o!'

In Lion's mouth was a live iguana, frantically struggling to get away. The dog went to Mr Gidharee and Mr Gidharee bent to take the bleeding iguana away from him. I could not watch. Just to see the iguana in Lion's mouth made me feel strange all over. I heard Mr Gidharee saying, as if to himself, 'It looks as if this boy don't like "guana".' Then he said, 'Lion, boy, when I tell people how you does hunt for me they doesn't believe, you know.' I glanced round to see what was happening and this time I all but fainted. He had taken off the iguana's head with his cutlass and the bleeding iguana was still whipping and struggling to get away. It seemed that its head was on the ground in the rice, for Lion was sniffing and yelping at something there.

'Where the others?' Mr Gidharee said to the dog. 'Go back, now. You is a good hunter. Go back with the rest now, Lion, boy.'

And then he said to me, 'Shell, boy, you don't know how sweet "guana" is. Boy, you don't know nothing – take it from me.'

I was looking away, still feeling upset. I heard him humming to himself and cutting up the iguana. He was taking the meat home to cook!

5

It was about a week afterwards, when, on coming out into the road I saw the *dougla* girl under the cashew tree. I walked towards the cashew tree to go down the hill to the shops. She was stooping and she had her dress fixed carefully to cover her knees and she appeared to be breaking off the nuts from the fallen cashews. As I passed she looked up and I said, 'Hello.'

'Hello: she said, and she smiled. I slowed down, and she said, 'You is the feller who went with Pa?'

'Yes. In Cedar Grove? Yes, that's me.'

'He was talking about you all the time,' she said. Her smile was very warm and there seemed to be laughter in her eyes.

'I had a nice time in Cedar Grove.'

'Everybody does have a nice time with Pa. Pa funny too bad.'

I was not going down to the shops for anything in particular. In fact, it was only when I had seen her that I had decided to walk down to the shops. Seeing how simple and easy-going she was, I was encouraged to stay and talk. I pretended to be calm but I was somewhat tense inside.

She had been gathering cashew nuts. Now she continued doing this, and everytime she stooped she carefully pulled down her dress over her knees.

'You not going to this Government School?' she said.

'Not yet.'

'Pa said you from Down-the-beach.'

'Aha.'

'Radix?'

'Yes.'

'So you going to the RC.'

'Aha.'

She had several nuts now in a heap on the ground, and now she stood up again and she was trying to wipe out the cashew stains from her hand. I was feeling awkward, with nothing to say, and I was just wondering whether I should go, when I saw someone like Lennard coming up the hill.

'Lennard coming,' I said.

She dashed to a tree and picked a leaf. She seemed suddenly full of play. She looked all around her and then she saw him coming, and she stood looking towards him, gigglingly, with both hands behind her back.

As Lennard drew near I saw that he had a whip in one hand and a leaf in the other. He, too, had the giggles. She said to me, 'We cut *green-leaf*.'

'Yes, I know.'

From the time she had dashed to get the leaf I had known what was going on, for we had this game at our school. Her face was bright with playfulness. For a moment I hated everything.

As Lennard came up he scrutinized her with his eyes. They were both grinning and she was holding up her green leaf in front of her, and as he had his own, neither of them bothered to say, 'Green-leaf!' Lennard raised his whip, jokingly, as if to hit her, and she jumped away and he tried to get hold of her but she slipped from him and ran a little way up the road. Then she broke off a hibiscus limb to threaten him with. As she came back again Lennard said to me, 'I didn't know you know Rosa.'

' "Rosa" for my friends,' she said, ' "Rosalie" to you – if you please.'

'She is a nice little jane,' Lennard said to me. 'Going to the school fair, Ro?'

'Look if you call me a nice jane again I'll go and tell Pa!'

'Don't bother about old man Gidharee,' he told me.

'But look at this boy!' Rosalie cried. 'Don't be fresh!'

'Set those dogs on him,' I joked.

'She wouldn't do that. Serious now, Rosa, you going to the fair Discovery Day?'

'All depends,' she said. 'You?'

'But sure,' Lennard said.

Rosalie turned to me: 'You?'

'Ah – yes,' I said. I did not even know about the fair.

Lennard had hardly taken his eyes off her since he had arrived. Now he said, 'All depends on what, Ro?'

'On if I feel like.'

'Well you better feel like!'

'Why? To please who?' She put her arms akimbo and tilted up her chin at him.

'To please *me*,' Lennard said.

'Ah, drop dead!'

Lennard made a grab for her and she scampered up the road. Then he left her alone.

She came back and she bent to pick up her heap of cashew nuts. She bent down most carefully and delicately. She was going to put the nuts in her dress, holding the front of her dress like a bowl, when, probably remembering us, she changed her mind. For she would have had to hold up the front of her dress a little, and she certainly would not want to do that with us there. She tried to scoop up the nuts with both hands, and finally getting all in, she stood up.

'See you, gentlemen,' she said.

'You calling *me*, gentleman?' Lennard said. 'Don't depend on that.'

'I'm not talking to *you*.'

'He is not any gentleman neither,' Lennard said. 'Boy, you is any gentleman?'

I just laughed.

Rosalie said: 'You is always some spokesman for somebody. Let him talk for himself. Anyway I must go. See you fellers.'

She skipped across the road.

Lennard said, 'Rosa.'

She stood up.

'Stay a little bit,' he said.

'For what?'

I could see Lennard wanted me to go away now. Rosalie stood looking at him with raised eyebrows, and he said nothing and I guessed it was because I was there. So I said, 'Look. I'll see you fellers some time,' and moved off.

I ambled down towards the shops.

6

It seemed like many days afterwards, when, on going out after the cashew, I saw Rosalie Gidharee in the road. She must have only just walked out of her gateway, for after a moment the brown dog, Lion, came springing out after her, frisking about and playing with her. She cried: 'Lion, stop! *Stop*! Stop it, Lion!' But the dog kept on frisking and growling and playing with her. She picked up a piece of twig from the roadside and Lion ran away.

'He only *playing* with you,' I said, from near the cashew tree. She did not quite hear me. I said it from there mainly to draw her away from her gateway, and towards where I was. She put her hands to her ears to show she did not hear.

'Come up here,' I said boldly.

She still did not hear but she began walking towards the cashew tree.

I had had a stone in my hand ready to pelt the cashew with, but I dropped this now and began thinking what to say to her. She was wearing a blue skirt and sailor bodice and she looked wonderful and new and strange. It was a brilliant morning, and behind her the drop of the hill was gradual, then severe, and the sun was just climbing the edge of the far trees.

She was near up now and she said, 'Sorry. Couldn't hear you. What's that you was saying?'

'The dog,' I said. 'Lion was only playing with you.'

'Oh, Lion. Lion too blinking frisky.'

I laughed. As she stood there she seemed so simple and pure. I supposed that as she said 'blinking' she thought she had said quite a lot. Her skirt was longish and I guessed it was her sister's. There was a big girl in their house and I reasoned this must be her sister. Rosalie had pulled in the skirt at the waist, to take up the slack, and had pinned it up. I was a bit surprised because she was not at all self-conscious, and yet other girls were always fussing about how they looked. I was glad to see her like this, with the long skirt, and the safety-pin showing. The bodice fitted neatly over her slightly-rising chest, and as I glanced over her, she seemed perfect in every way.

Her eyes were not on me now, but on the ground. She was looking for cashew nuts. She walked around, pouncing whenever she saw a cashew, and my eyes followed her. Then abruptly she said: 'Why you don't pelt your cashew.'

'Why?'

'Don't bother about me. Pelt your cashew.'

I was embarrassed. I said nothing. I just stood looking at her, pretending to be puzzled.

She said: 'Or if you want me to go – '

'You don't have to go, Rosalie.'

She turned looking at me in the same way she had looked at Lennard that time when he had asked her to stay. She knew she was pretty. She knew we were all frantic over her. I cursed myself for letting her see how silly I was.

After a while I said, 'Where's Lennard? I ain't seen him for days.'

'Somewhere around, perhaps.'

'He ain't come up to see you?' I felt my voice tremble.

'To see me? Why?'

And then with sudden rashness, I said, 'Well, you is his jane.'

To my surprise she still stood there. She did not storm away. She looked at me calmly and said, '*His* jane? Lennard only fresh!'

I was suddenly relieved that she was not angry, and then even more relieved by what she had said. Now she looked up in my face and slanted her head, and her arms were akimbo. 'He told you that?'

'No. Oh no. I just said that.'

'What make you say that'

'Just pulling your legs.'

'He *said* it. O God, boy, just tell me if he really said that!'

'No, not really. I was only making a little joke with you.'

'Well that's a funny kinda joke to make,' she said.

Presently, she seemed to forget all about it, and she began looking up at the ripe cashews on the tree.

'Oo,' she said, 'look at that nice one up there.'

'I'll pick it for you.'

'Not for me. I don't like cashew. Not these. These too *rack*.'

'I'll pick it for you for the nut.'

'Oh, not so much trouble for that little nut!'

'I'll pelt it down anyway.'

I started pelting again. As I pelted I was thinking of lots of things and I was not really caring for the cashew. I was thinking about Joe and Rosalie and I wondered if I should ask her about Joe. I thought I'd better not. I thought of Lennard and how she had reacted about him, and then other things came to mind. Then all of a sudden that big poster on the shop down the hill came to mind and it was about the Discovery Day fair. It was stuck against the shop and it said in fancy lettering: GRAND DISCOVERIE FAYRE AND DANCE. This had stirred me mainly because of the quaintness of the writing and because Rosalie and Lennard had talked about the fair. I turned round to Rosalie and found her looking at me.

'So Monday's the fair?'

'Oh gosh, yes. Yes. You going?'

'Don't know, really. You?'

'Yes. Come on, boy – why not?'

'I mighn't be able to come.'

'Why?'

'Pa might be going to hospital,' I said, and a wave of sadness swept upon me.

'What happen?'

'Pa sick. Bad.'

'I know. My Pa was saying something about that. Sorry.'

I said nothing, but looked the other way towards the hill. This was one of chose horrible moments of grief that now and again broke over me. My father's suffering hurt me greatly. No doctor seemed able to cure him. Instead of getting better he worsened every day.

'He'll be all right,' Rosalie said. 'For all you know he'll be soon all right. You know what I mean. I mean I know how you feeling.'

I was still looking towards the hills. I bit my lips and there was a little burning in my nose.

'Don't worry,' she said, 'he'll get better.'

I stood silent.

As old as I was, often when I thought of Pa's illness, I lost all calmness. Now I was holding the tears at bay, and the phase was passing. I heard a deep bark and I looked round and it was Rover who had come out into the road. Seeing Rosalie he scampered towards her. Before he reached her she cried: 'Rover! Look here, *Rover!*' Rover stopped short and he seemed to understand that she did not want to play. He looked up at her, wagging his tail. I was feeling better now. 'Rove,' I said. He wagged his tail more violently but he did not come. He was wanting to frolic with Rosalie. But she was not in the mood.

'Rover feeling frisky,' I said.

'I'll give him "frisky",' she said.

Rover stood up in front of her, looking up at her. She said sternly: 'You better go back inside, eh!'

He still stood there, wagging his tail and his whole bottom.

I said, 'So you old man stayed home today, Rosalie?'

'Yes.'

I had reasoned that out because of the dogs. Mr Gidharee never went to Cedar Grove without those dogs. Having seen Lion and Rover I knew he was at home. I was sure that Tiger, the lazy one, was sunning himself somewhere.

'You all doesn't keep those dogs tied?'

'Sometimes. Not always.'

'You never know, you know. If anybody just wander in your yard, they could be dangerous.'

'That's why we have them,' she said, 'that's just why.'

I laughed. I said, 'Four good Tobago dogs – major!'

' "*Good* Tobago dogs? You mean "good-for-nothing"!'

'That is four *good* dogs,' I said, seriously, 'four champion dogs. Anybody could see that.'

'Maybe,' she said casually. '*We* like them, anyway.'

She did not have the cashew nuts in her hands now and I did

not know what she had done with them. She had gathered a few when she had first come. I only thought of this now as she moved off to go. Although my mind was not quite free of my father, I felt a certain pain on account of her, too.

She said, 'Think I'm going in – else Dolly will start screaming for me like mad.'

'Oh, that girl is your sister?'

'Yes – you like her?'

'Not her, somebody else.'

She pretended she did not hear. 'Think I'm going in, boy'

'All right, Rosalie Gidharee.'

'And what's your other name – I don't mean "Shellie", I mean, Shellie what?'

'Shellie anything you like.'

'Okay Mr Anything-you-like,' she said; and she went in.

7

Discovery Day was the first time I went inside the Mayaro Government School. It stood on Police Station Hill, where the hill joined the road to the beach. When I arrived there, crowds had already lined the stairway, waiting to get inside.

Most of these boys and girls I did not know, for I was still new to Pierre Hill. They milled their way up the stairs, impatient to get inside. The girls brightened the place with their gay dresses and they looked very strange and exciting. I pressed along with the crowd and at the same time I was keeping a sharp look-out for Rosalie.

It took a long while to get up the stairway and into the

veranda, but once there, I quickly got out my ticket and slid inside.

Here, the place was a vast hall and there seemed to be hundreds of school-children about, and there was a steady roar from the amount of talking. There was a stage at one end of the hall, and the musicians were here and getting out their instruments from huge clumsy boxes, and laughing and talking. After a while they began tuning up with blasts of music and this promptly drew people to the front of the stage. Everyone seemed anxious for the dance to begin.

There was no sign of Rosalie yet and I was keeping a watch on the stream of boys and girls pouring in through the door. It did not seem that she could have slipped in without my seeing. I wanted to see when she came in for fear that I'd lose her in this vast crowd.

Outside the school there was a sports ground and today the Mayaro Athletic Club was holding a sports meeting there. I remembered this when I heard the roar outside and now I went to the window to look. The ground was like a football field, but by drawing lanes round it for the long distance races they had made it look oval, and they had drawn lanes across it for the hundred-yards event. They had not yet started the flat races and the commotion was at the greasy pole. A man was trying to climb it and every time he got within touching distance of the prizes, he slid right back down again. There was a lot of people at the fence near the pole, willing the man up, and there were people standing on a lorry in the main road and looking over to see.

I was not interested in the sports and I was only looking out because of the roar outside. When I turned round again there were a great many more people inside the school, and I suddenly became fearful that Rosalie may have come in while I was looking outside. Still, if she did she'd be around somewhere. It was very hot and I was careful to wipe my face as I did not want my face to be shiny now. I still watched the doorway for Rosalie.

Although the fair was mainly for children there were a number of grown people here too, and most of the men were at the bar. I was looking at those at the bar and at the way their eyes shone when they put the glasses to their heads, and at the way their smiles lit up – when all of a sudden I jumped. Two hands had clamped down over my eyes. I held them and struggled to push them off, and I bent and twisted and finally I managed to ease them away and swung round to see who had held me.

'Boy, you so coward – look how frighten he was!' Lennard said, laughing.

'You always blinking well playing the fool!' I said heatedly. I was really annoyed. I did not want my clothes rumpled or rubbed upon. I had tried hard to look nice today, and to smell sweet, and I did not want Lennard to rub up on me. He saw I was annoyed and he was highly amused at this, and he said: 'So you vex then, old man!'

'You always doing that I said, 'you always doing this stupid thing!'

'All right, you looking nice,' he said. 'Everybody know you looking nice.'

'Don't be silly.'

He came up to straighten back my tie and I let him, and he fixed my collar properly, and he said, 'She bound to fall for you today.'

'Fall for who! You mean fall for you.' I had softened a little.

After doing these little things and smoothing me out again he moved back a few steps to look at me. He was grinning and well satisfied. 'Oh, God, you'll take the little jane today,' he cried, 'you looking *nice* boy.' He came up to me and rested his hand on my shoulder. 'You looking major, man, *major*.'

'You looking all right too,' I said.

It was not just to please him that I said this. It was the first time I had seen him dressed up and he looked smart and strange. He was wearing one of those knitted 'schoolboy' ties – something I had always wanted – and I was a little jealous in a way.

After a little while Rosalie came to mind again and I forgot about the tie. The view to the doorway was completely blocked now and I began feeling uneasy. I was just thinking of moving to some other part, when the first set struck up.

Lennard wheeled round and straightaway started looking for a girl to dance with. The whole place had sprung to life. They were playing a break-away calypso and the floor was already swarming with dancers.

I lost Lennard for a moment and when I spotted him again he had already got hold of a partner and he was dancing so funny he made me laugh. It was just that he wasn't shy in the least. He was letting go of the girl and spinning, and spinning the girl also, and then holding her again and dancing with his bottom sticking out. He turned round, perhaps to look for me, and he saw me laughing and he made a sign towards where there was a knot of girls. He meant for me to go and ask for a set. I was really feeling to dance but I did not know the girls and I hesitated. Lennard danced himself near to me, and he said: 'What happen, you is a wall-flower or something? Why you don't dance, boy.'

The girl dancing with him was smiling in agreement.

I said, 'Dance with who? You?'

The girl nearly choked with laughter.

Lennard said, 'What's wrong with you! Look at all those girls over there! Girls like peas!'

'I don't even know them.'

They both laughed at my silliness. He was dancing his partner right next to me, to talk to me. He said, 'Well I never! So you have to *know* girls to dance with them and all?'

His partner whispered: 'Leave the boy alone. He shy.'

At that moment I had to move out of the way as I was obstructing other dancers. A lot of couples had been bouncing into Lennard while he danced stationary, next to me, and he was getting very angry stares. I slipped back towards the wall.

I stood up near the benches. Then I began to strengthen myself to go to the knot of girls to ask for a dance. And then I thought, next set – for this one was bound to be nearly over. Suddenly, there came a swell of cheering from the sportsground and I made for the window. As I weaved my way to the window someone said, 'Shell!'

I turned round. 'Oh hel-lo!' I said. My heart had given a great heave. 'Hello Rosalie. Hi Joe.'

Joe was holding her close, dancing with her. He was dancing very coolly, hardly moving. Rosalie was wearing a smart pink dress, with a cream dress-band, and she had two large pink bows in her hair. She looked breath-taking, and when I reached the window and leaned against it I could hear my heart thumping against the wood.

I turned round to look at them. They had hardly moved from that spot. As the music warmed up everybody seemed to be going wild, but Joe and Rosalie were hardly moving. Rosalie was looking up into his face.

I felt something very like pain. Then I lost them as people danced across my view. I felt certain now that there was something between Rosalie and Joe.

I tried not to feel depressed. I liked Joe and I wished I did not feel so awful over Rosalie. My eyes searched the crowd but there was no sign of them.

As soon as the set stopped I spotted them in a far corner of the hall. As I was walking towards them I came across Lennard and the same girl he had been dancing with.

He said: 'I was just coming to look for you. You dance at all yet?'

'No.'

'Okay – you could dance the next set with Joan.'

I was suddenly embarrassed and I did not know what to say, and as the girl herself said nothing, I looked at Lennard and said, 'Why?'

'Don't be silly. Joan is my friend. She'll dance with you.'

The girl looked at him rather sternly and said, 'The boy wants to get partners for his own self. You can't tell him who to dance with.' She was a round-faced, pleasant-looking girl, and her saying this made me feel even more embarrassed.

Lennard was going to say something, but he stopped. He looked around for a moment, then he said to me, 'Where you off to?'

'Nowhere. Just over here.'

Lennard said to the girl: 'Joan, just a minute. Wait here for me.'

He took me across to the window. As we walked, he said, 'Look, if I offer you the girl to dance you ain't have to say a damn thing – you just have to dance. Girls funny, boy. By the way, see Rosalie?'

'Yes. She and Joe was dancing. They at the other end.'

'That girl like Joe bad, boy. Met her on the stairs coming in. First person she ask for was Joe.'

'Yes. I know.'

Looking out through the window he said, '*First* person the little jane ask for! Jesus Christ!' And he shook his head and laughed.

'And the second person she asked for?'

'Well she didn't ask about you if you want to know.'

'Not me, boy. That is between you and Joe.'

'But the little jane love him bad,' he said.

Lennard had spoken as if it had finally come home to him that those two were in love. He did not seem at all bitter or disappointed, and I was surprised. He looked so friendly and cheerful, even gentle, quite unlike that first time I had met him on Pierre Hill. Now he was looking towards the other end of the hall to see if he could spot them and I did not know if he saw them at all but he said, 'That Joe is a sharp-shooter!' and we laughed.

As we were talking a new set started up and the place was suddenly alive, and Lennard took me by the arm and said, 'Come!' Quickly he found Joan and he just said, 'Okay, dance,' leaving us together, and disappeared. I looked at Joan's face and she was very pleasant and ready to dance. I held her, and for a moment I was a little flustered, not sure which foot to start off with. Then I listened for what the music was playing and it was a rhumba, and I said, shame-facedly, 'Can't dance a rhumba too good, you know.'

'Doesn't matter,' she said. 'I can't dance, anyway. So.'

They were playing *Peanut Vendor*, and *Peanut Vendor* was the easiest rhumba in the world to dance to and I did not know what had come over me and made me say I could not dance a rhumba. The music was clear and sweet, with the drums distinct, and this rhumba in particular always went to my head. I held Joan not too tight, not too loose, and we were already going good.

'Who's playing this, I mean, what band this is?' I said. The music was slowly intoxicating me and I was beginning to feel nice.

'Al Timothy.'

'Oh, Al Timothy. O God!'

They were playing *Peanut Vendor* hysterically sweet. I lost all shyness. I held Joan and danced her close, then I held her out and spun her once, twice, then I myself spun once, twice, and I made the side-step and came in to her, and she side-stepped and wheeled round and then I held her close again. I looked at her and her face was bright and full and you could see she was enjoying herself. I let her go so I could try the cake-walk and it was so funny she broke down laughing. The cake-walk was something you did only in the jive but sometimes it could be done in the rhumba and I had done it many times myself. Then I started all over again and this time I held her close and my cheek was against her temple.

Al Timothy's trombonist was playing like an angel. I was beginning to feel a little moisture inside my shirt and I held Joan off a little and I looked down at her face.

'Warm, Joan?'

'If!'

Nothing could be done about the heat. All the windows were already open. In a crowd like this it was bound to be steaming hot.

'O God, Joan, that trombonist, eh! You like it?'

'Major!' she said.

I tried all the steps I knew, for although the place was crowded you could still try your steps. I held her close, cheek-to-cheek, and every now and then when the music was too much for me, I let her go and did my pretty things. I was doing them now and she looked highly delighted and amused and I held her in again and I squeezed her a little. She looked up into my face: 'And you said you couldn't rhumba!'

'What to do. I have to try, mammie, O God!'

It was as though I was going delirious. It was a long time since last I had enjoyed a dance like that. I felt half of it was due to Joan herself. She was plump, but a good mover, and so soft to the touch. She was not flashy in her movements, yet in her gentle, quiet way, she was most exciting.

'You from up here? Pierre Hill? Or, rather, Mayaro, on the whole?'

'Yes – and no,' she said.

'That is Japanese. I can't understand that.'

She laughed. 'Well I'm on holiday here. I'm from Sangre.'

'Oh, I see. How come Lennard know you?'

'Oh, I'm staying at the Maynards'. He's always there.'

'The Maynards? You know I don't even know the Maynards?'

The music seemed to be sending me haywire. I looked to see who was playing that trombone. I said. 'O God, I love that trombone!' I spun Joan once, twice, three times, then I let her sail back to me.

'Sangre Grande seems a nice place,' I said.

'You know there?'

'No. It looks nice on the map.'

She thought I was trying to be funny, but I wasn't. On the map of Trinidad, County St Andrew was always in a very pleasant green, and Sangre Grande was dotted right in the north-east corner of it. It always looked nice to me.

I said, 'But my father used to work up there.'

'Where?'

'You know that big junction – after you turn off from Cocal?'

'That is North Manzanilla,' she said. She was quietly amused.

'I like there,' I said.

The music had now gone very delicate, and I was making very delicate steps, and Joan, looking at me, said again, 'Boy, you said you couldn't rhumba!'

I laughed.

'Why?' She seemed quite impressed.

'I don't know.'

'Yes, but I mean – '

'Girl, I can't dance any rhumba. I only trying, mammie-o.'

Just as the music was getting me mad it stopped suddenly, and people roared appreciation for the band.

I thought of getting Joan a seat before the crowd rushed back to the benches. It was difficult wading through that melee. I was considering whether I should stay talking to her or whether I should go away. Because of the dancing I had taken a sudden liking to her and really I wished to stay talking with her. Only that if you stayed talking with a girl between sets she got the idea you were waiting for the next dance and that you wanted to monopolise her. I happened to see a spare space on the benches and I took Joan to it. Then I left her and went to the window to see how the sports were going.

I had thought of the sports because while we were dancing there had been a continuous uproar outside. Now as I looked out the crowd was on its toes. The Ladies' hundred-yards event was in its closing stages. The roar and laughter of the crowd drowned out the voice on the public address system and it looked very like pandemonium there below. I did not see much of the race and presently it was all over, and the crowd was still in uproar and you could hear the commentator shouting to get himself heard. As I was straining to hear what he was saying I felt a touch on my shoulder.

I turned round. 'Oh, hello, Joe boy,' I said, surprised.

'Looking for you all over the place.'

'Oh – me? Why?'

'No, just so. We saw you one time, and then you just melt. That's all.'

'Where's Rosalie?'

'Somewhere about.'

'Somewhere about? You mean you don't know where your own jane is?'

'Boy, she isn't my girl, boy. She was just dancing with Lennard that last set.'

Oh, I thought, so Lennard's still after old Rosalie! No wonder he left Joan with me! But I knew it was not really so. Really, he had given me Joan because he wanted me to have somebody to dance with – because I did not know any of the girls.

'I was dancing with Joan,' I said.

'Which Joan?'

'Oh, you don't know Joan.' I looked across the hall. Joan was still sitting there, but with so many people passing to and fro it was difficult to point her out to him.

'I'll show you later,' I said, 'she's a girl from Sangre Grande. Lennard friend.'

'Oh, that girl. With Sheila Maynard. Oh I know that girl. She's nice.'

'Boy!'

'She's a nice little thing. Want a drink?'

'What kind?' I looked at him. Somehow I didn't expect Joe to be talking about drinks, let alone nice women.

'Something to make us merry,' he said.

'Try your luck. Bet they won't serve us any strongs.'

'How much you want to bet? You know who you talking to? Come on, let's find Lennard.'

I followed him, weaving through the crowd. I was quite amused about Joe. I said to myself, Well look at Joe talking about drinks. Who could beat that!

Before we got very far a set struck up and the floor was again crowded with dancers. I was feeling bright at the prospect of having a drink at the bar – if they'd serve us – and at the same time there was the faint thought of Rosalie at the back of my mind. This band, Al Timothy, was again playing very good. They had a very good trombonist, and the man on the bass was no fool either. As I wove through behind Joe I kept thinking of the string of lovely girls here at Pierre Hill whom I had never seen before. Lucky thing I came to the fair, I thought.

I suddenly wanted to see Rosalie very much. Joe was looking around, trying to spot Lennard. I felt certain Lennard was dancing with Rosalie somewhere in this crowd. But as we got down to the other end of the room, there was Rosalie walking towards us.

'Long time no see,' she said. 'You hiding yourself or something?' She seemed glad to see me.

'Me?' I said.

'Yes, you. I ain't seeing you at all.'

'I was at the other end.'

Joe said, 'He was looking at the sports.'

She glared at Joe, 'You – don't talk about *you* at all!'

'What's wrong now?' he said.

'You think you could just walk away and leave people and now you saying what wrong now?'

'Well Lennard came and ask you for a dance. I couldn't stand up there and wait.'

She said nothing. She was giving him a really withering look. I felt certain that there was something between them. At least, on Rosalie's side. Joe did not seem to me to care very much. But he knew she liked him.

I turned to Rosalie, 'Where's Lennard now?'

'Don't know.'

'Joe want to buy us a drink.'

She made a sneering little laugh. Then she looked at him from the corners of her eyes. You could see from her ways how much she cared for him, and how glad she was to be near him. Joe paid her no mind and she said, 'Don't bother with *him*. Playing big man to go and drink at bar!'

I said, 'Don't worry, they wouldn't serve us.'

'Why not?' Joe said. 'Let's find Len and you'll see.'

Rosalie nudged me and said, 'That's all some people does think about – *drink*.'

'All right, Gidharee,' Joe said.

'Don't be fresh!' she said.

Joe walked away, still searching for Lennard, and he signalled me on, but I stayed talking to Rosalie. She was looking most desirable and I was feeling badly seeing her throw herself at Joe like that. All she wanted to do now was to talk about Joe, and I talked a little and then I fell into silence. We both looked at the people dancing and then the set finished and people were pouring back to the benches.

'So how you enjoying the fair?' I said.

'Great, boy. That was the only set I didn't dance.'

'This is a nice fête. How about some ice-cream, Rose?'

'Oh, sorry, but while ago I make Joe buy me a big cream. I mean, don't feel – '

'No, it's all right.'

'How about you – *you* enjoying yourself?'

'Yes, girl. I like this fête.'

'And just fancy you looking at sport.'

'No, I was dancing too.'

'Oh yes?'

'Yes, man, I was dancing. You know Joan – look, that girl in the pink dress over there. Over there, by the stage.'

'Oh I see. Oh yes. Very nice. Congrats.' She was laughing.

'What's all this congrats for?'

'You is a devil on the level. Not a bad jane, though.'

'First time I ever see the girl in my life.'

Her face was all mischief. 'You is a genius,' she said.

'What's wrong with you. I was just dancing with the girl just so. Lennard introduced me. You see *you* wouldn't give me a dance so I have to see what I could do.'

'You joking, of course.'

'Not really.'

'Well you never ask me for a dance.'

'Okay, well I ask you now.'

I felt my voice tremble in saying that. Standing so close to her and looking at her I remembered Lennard saying how he liked *dougla* girls more than anything. Joe, whom she liked did not seem to care about girls at all. To me, Lennard just made a big noise, he wasn't at all serious. Neither of them had any idea how much I liked Rosalie. Not even Rosalie herself, although she must have guessed something by now. A new set was about to start up, and having already asked for the dance, I looked at her now and I said, 'Okay?'

'Sure,' she said, 'once it isn't a fox-trot.'

'All right.'

I stood there, excited, and my heart was racing. I was thinking of the moment when I would be putting my arm about her. I was feeling a thrill just to think of it. Apart from her quaintness, she was looking a great deal more developed than she looked, normally, and I guessed it was because she was dressed up. I looked at her and we smiled, and inside my heart felt ablaze.

8

When the band struck up I waited a few seconds to hear what they were playing then I took her hand. They were playing *One Day When We Were Young*, and I could see she was working out what sort of dance it was.

'I like this waltz, Rose – you?'

She smiled.

This waltz seemed to bring the whole crowd onto the floor. I tried to manoeuvre for space, I was so overwhelmed by having my arms around Rosalie that it was a few moments before I was going well.

But I was soon going well. Al Timothy seemed to be playing this with a strange, unearthly beauty, and the music seemed to be seeping into me. I held Rosalie close as we made the one-two-three, one-two-three, and I looked down on her face. Her eyes were bright and alive and there was the mischievous twitch round her mouth.

She said, 'You enjoying it?'

'I enjoying it bad, girl.'

The windows were all open because it was so crowded and hot, and through the windows were the fronds of the coconut palms outside. The winds were rustling them and they seemed to be waltzing with us. The trumpeter of Al Timothy came to the end of a bar and trailed off into silence.

For a moment the music was only on the drums, and then came the first sweet bars of *The Tennessee Waltz*.

'*Tennessee Waltz*,' I said, 'O God! *Tennessee Waltz*, Ro!'

Rosalie looked up at me and laughed. She probably thought me a little crazy. I was dancing her cool, taking advantage of whatever space there was. There was not much space for the floor was crowded too thickly, and I had to make turns well within myself. My cheek was against her temple and the smell of her hair was of bay rum and coconut oil, and somehow this made me very tender towards her. I held her softly, and secretly I imagined she belonged to me.

I could judge now that she liked dancing cool. You could always tell what a girl liked by what she was inclined to do. Sometimes you wanted to dance cool and your partner wanted more action and she was almost breaking away from your arms. You could tell Rosalie liked it really cool. She was not doing much for herself and perhaps she was not a good dancer, but she was what people called 'light'. I treasured her for his.

The Al Timothy trombonist was playing *The Tennessee Waltz* so sweetly he made me feel to cry. As I danced, pressing Rosalie to me, I could feel straps at her back. I listened to the trombonist, and I joined him, singing to myself, '. . . I remember the night, and the Tennessee Waltz . . .' Rosalie looked up into my face. She was amused. 'This boy really having a good time,' she said.

'Gosh, this *Tennessee Waltz*, girl. This *Tennessee Waltz* could kill me.'

'You is a good dancer,' she said.

'Don't bother with you!'

'No, I mean it.'

'Well if I is a good dancer that's a miracle because all the dance I does ever go to is the RC School bazaars.'

'You is a good dancer,' she said.

Every now and again cheers from the sports-ground outside came into the school. Sometimes it was a roar and sometimes it was just people shouting.

'You like dancing, Rosalie?'

'Sometimes. You?'

'Yes – O God!'

'I could see that.'

I could tell by the change in the music that the set was coming to an end. I began dancing Rosalie to the corner where she had been sitting.

'You could dance nice, man,' she said.

'That's what Joan said.'

'Aha? Things going nice? You still thinking about your Little Joan, eh?'

'Thinking about *you*.'

My heart was quivering. She did not speak.

'Eh?' I said.

' "Eh" about what?'

'Thinking about you.'

'That's nice,' she said coldly, 'much obliged.'

I felt pain. I was embarrassed and ashamed and I did not know where to turn my face. After a moment our eyes met and to my great surprise her face had a very pleased look. Right away I thought I'd press on, for if what I'd said pleased her there must be a good chance for me here. I wanted to tell her I loved her. I wanted to be quick, before the set finished. I thought of Joe but I did not feel guilty because I was sure Joe could not be bothered about any girl. There were boys like that and you did not have to know them too long to find out. I framed words to say, and now, as I opened my mouth to speak, Rosalie said: 'What about your Pa – he all right?'

'Not really.'

'No?'

The set stopped and we were in the middle of a stampede.

When I got Rosalie to her place Joe was sitting there. He got up to give her the seat, and Rosalie said, Thanks for keeping the seat for me – or some such thing, and she seemed to be melting to jelly for him.

Joe was in a hurry. He held my sleeves. 'Come, Len by the bar. We'll get the drinks.'

I said, 'See you,' to Rosalie.

'You drunkards!' she said. She tried to raise a laugh but she was really disappointed that Joe was going away again.

When we got to the bar, there was Lennard straining his neck looking out for us. I had not seen him for about a whole hour. He looked really smart in that knitted 'schoolboy' tie, and that cream shirt.

He said: 'So what happening, man, how's tricks? I hear you on top the world.'

'What's all this about?'

'Rumours,' he said, 'rumours are flying.' Then he punched me playfully on my chest, 'I only pulling your legs, boy, don't worry. You dance with Joan all right?'

'Oh yes. Thanks a lot. You is a good feller.'

'Christ! I ain't *give* her to you. I only *lend* you a dance, boy. You is a chicken-hawk or what!'

The others laughed.

'Anyway she's a nice girl,' I said.

'You telling me!' Lennard said. Then he said seriously, 'Joan is plenty girl. Plenty, plenty girl.'

He went up to the bar-counter now and raised his brows to the bar-man and the bar-man gave a slight nod. He had already spoken to the bar-man about the drinks. Lennard was taller than either Joe or me and he could have passed for eighteen without too much trouble. Joe and I were obviously under age. We had all drawn up to the bar, beside Lennard. The bar-man went on attending to a few people and when he was finished he came to Lennard and said, 'What you having, Sport?' He kept his voice low.

'Four rums,' Lennard whispered, 'with a little lime, please, Freddie?'

The bar-man turned away.

I was so impressed by Lennard's actually asking for *rum* at a bar that it did not sink into me that he had said *four* rums. It was only when the bar-man brought the glasses and I looked round that I saw another boy on the bench with Joe.

This was the boy who had been with them when I had first seen them pelting cashew on Pierre Hill. When I caught his eye I gave him a nod of the head and he did the same and smiled. Lennard was leaning, against the counter watching the bar-man do the rum-and-limes and I was beside him.

The bar-man was making the mixtures very delicately, pouring just the right amount of lime.

I said, 'Boy, he is a *chemist*.'

Lennard looked at me, 'Don't sweet-talk the man. That won't get you no place.'

The bar-man had smiled.

Then Lennard turned to me again, 'No, Freddie is all right. He is a nice feller. He'll give me any drink I ask for.'

'Oh you know him,' I whispered.

'Oh yes. Everybody know Freddie. That's one of my real good pals. A dam nice feller.

He was talking just loud enough for the bar-man to hear what he was saying. The bar-man finished the drinks then passed two glasses to us, then passed the other two.

'Not true, Fred?' Lennard turned to him, 'I was telling this man you'd serve anybody a drink. You don't humbug nobody.'

'I don't humbug nobody,' Freddie said. He spoke slowly and rather gravely. He was not a full man. He was at that stage where a boy had just become a man. He thought a little and then he went on. 'Once a feller *discreet* and don't get me in trouble I'll serve him. It's not my business if he under age.'

'See what I mean?' Lennard said to me.

The other two had come up now for their drinks and we all touched glasses.

'Cheers,' Lennard called to Freddie and put the glass to his lips.

'Cheers,' Freddie said, although he wasn't drinking. And then he brightened a little and said, 'I know you boys a bit young, but I know how it is. I meself can't dance without a few in – meself.'

Lennard approved of him very much, and of all he was saying, and they were soon deep in conversation. The new fellow, whom I had seen pelting cashew, was sipping silently, on his own, and I jerked my head back, meaning him to come over. He came and we started talking but he was very dull. He wanted me to do all the talking. After a while I lost interest in him and started listening to the roars from the sports-ground outside.

Things seemed exciting out there but I did not feel to go to the window to look. I turned round to Freddie and Lennard talking. Lennard saw me look, and tilting his chin towards me, said to Freddie, 'This is Gidharee son-in-law, you know.'

They both burst out laughing, and Joe, who had been standing by, just listening, smiled.

'Oh, yes?' Freddie said, 'He's a lucky man. Some fellers just born with their own luck, eh!'

I said, 'Don't bother with Lennard.'

They had all taken it as a joke and I took it as a joke, myself. Then Lennard said to Freddie, 'He's a new feller up here. From Radix.'

'I think I see him before, but I can't place him,' Freddie said, then under his breath he said to Lennard, 'shy like hell.'

'Who shy!' I said.

'Well you is a *young* feller, anyway.'

'Not me. I ain't shy.'

We had all drunken up and refilled now and Lennard wanted to buy yet another round but I did not want any more. I looked around the hall which was bright with the coloured streamers. There were tinsels hanging from the streamers and there were large blue paper-bells hanging in the middle of the ceiling. The sun outside was bright on the coconut fronds and between the spaces, and the way the coconut trunks criss-crossed one another made the place look crazy. I was feeling light and happy. At the moment there was jiving going on in the hall and it seemed to make me giddy just to look on. I laughed.

Freddie, the bar-man, said, 'One gone.'

I looked at him. The others were laughing.

'What wrong!' I said. I said it rather sternly, in fact I almost shouted it. My own voice surprised me. The boys just kept on laughing and looking at me, and Freddie said again, 'One gone!'

So I started to laugh too and this brought roars of laughter from the others. The dancers looked so giddy it was as if they would fall over. They seemed to be reeling into me, and even though I moved a little, they all seemed as though they would crash into me. Bursts of cheering from the sports-ground kept rushing through the window. The school looked crazy with the ribbons of the girls.

'. . . Is all right, he wouldn't make no trouble,' I heard Lennard saying. Apparently he was talking to Freddie.

Freddie saw me looking and he turned his eyes towards Joe, pretending he was not talking about me. Still looking at Joe, he said, 'I ain't 'fraid for him. Once a man discreet, that's all. But for *Christ* sake don't give him no more drinks!'

I looked at each of them in turn and I looked at them very hard. Freddie had just replenished their glasses, and Lennard, Joe, and the other one were all sipping but not taking their eyes off me. Every now and again Joe was in such fits of laughter that he couldn't drink. Somehow the whole situation amused me and I started laughing hysterically. Torrents of laughter poured from Lennard and Freddie. Oddly enough, Joe stopped laughing now and he came over and put his hand on my shoulder. I became serious again and I looked at them all in turn, then I looked over my shoulder at Joe to see what the hell he was up too.

'What the hell happening here?' I said, 'what the bleddy hell happening here!'

Laughter rang out.

I looked round the bar. There were a lot of other people standing around, looking at what, I did not know.

'For God sake, what the hell you people want?' I cried.

I looked to Freddie for support but he was round the bar and was looking quite agitated. He was whispering to Lennard, and he made a sign at Joe, who had his arm around my neck. The only other thing I remember is the struggling with Lennard and Joe and Freddie, and Freddie blasting under his breath, saying that was the reason he didn't like to serve little boys with drinks. And then there was Joe on one side and Lennard on the other, holding me, and there was no struggling. And then there was Rosalie. And there was Freddie saying, Pass through the side door. Hold him straight. Do as if nothing ain't happen. And I remember the boys leading me up Pierre Hill, with my knees feeling funny, and the wind seeming to blow me about. And as far as I could tell, the rest was a blank, until I woke up that next bright day.

9

Discovery Day was well past before I saw Rosalie again, and the reason why I did not see her – nor see any of the boys – was because my father had taken worse and I had to be in the house. We had had a few terrifying weeks and there were many times when my mother had cried out in the night, thinking my father was dead. But he rallied on. The district doctor had recommended that he should go to the Colonial Hospital in Port-of-Spain, but my mother had resisted it all the time. Now, seeing no sign of recovery for him, she had agreed, and on this very day the ambulance had come for him.

We had many people in the house who had come to console my mother. They did not know us very well but on hearing of the illness they had come. My mother was greatly comforted. Mr Gidharee had called during the morning and he had said he was very sorry to hear, and that he'd send the wife over later. And in the afternoon both Mrs Gidharee and Rosalie had come.

Mrs Gidharee was a large-boned, stout lady, with a very round and contented-looking face, and she was *creole* – as Mr Gidharee had said. My mother took to her right away and they started talking. Rosalie looked very pleased to see me again, and for my part, I was touched that she should come to our house.

After her mother and mine had got into conversation, Rosalie came over to me. 'So how's things, Shell?'

'Okay.' That was the oddest question she could ask, at a time like this.

'I ain't see you since Discovery,' she said.

She smiled at this and I supposed she expected me to be amused. That was the day Lennard and Joe had brought me home drunk. I remembered it, of course, but I was much too overwrought to giggle over it. I said, 'No. Not since then.'

'You see Lennard and Joe since?'

'No.'

'That was a fête, eh!'

'I can't think about fête,' I said, not very kindly. I did not want to hurt her but I did not wish to talk about fêtes now.

'Cheer up,' she said.

'I can't think of that kind of thing now.'

'I know, but cheer up.'

I said nothing. My inside seemed to become soft and melting again. I bit my lips. I felt on the point of tears.

'Look how upset he is!' Rosalie said.

I was going to say that I was all right but if I had opened my mouth I would have broken down. My eyes brimmed over and as I raised my hand to wipe it I could not help crying.

Rosalie was silent. She came and stood up right next to where

I was sitting, and I guessed she was looking down at me. My mother, who was in the kitchen with Mrs Gidharee, heard me and came up the steps.

'What happen to you,' she said. 'What you crying for?'

This caused the complete breaking down and I could not control myself.

'What you crying for?' she said. 'You father gone to hospital – he ain't *dead*.'

Mrs Gidharee came in too. She was very calm. She said to my mother, 'His heart full. That must happen. It's natural, you know. You must try to console him.'

'I tired speaking to this boy,' my mother said. I could hear a peculiar wavering in her voice. 'This is not time to cry for you father. What in the name of God wrong with you?' And having said this, she herself burst into tears.

The Gidharees spent a long time with us, bringing us back to reason. Then when everything was as normal as could be, they slipped away. The evening fell silent and sombre. I sat down in the sitting room – which we called the hall – and my mother was in the bedroom and there was not a sound. I got up and stood up at the front door and looked outside. There was a big mango tree beside our house and it stood green and quiet, its leaves gently shaking in the wind. The lime tree in the yard had little fruit upon it. In the sky there was hardly any cloud. The peace and silence was like desolation.

I went down the steps and walked out into the road. There was nothing to see except a few dogs lying on the warm pitch. There was hardly anybody about. The cashew tree looked battered and empty and there were many brown leaves among the green. I walked down towards the cashew tree.

There was no fruit on the tree now, and, underneath, the last of the dropped fruit had rotted and dried. I sat down on the bank next to the tree, my feet in the drain.

I had my head in my hands and I was thinking. I was thinking of my father, whose ambulance must already be in Port-of-Spain. He had never looked quite so ill before. I did not know what was going to be. I felt dismal and afraid.

I sat there and a few people passed by in the road but I did not raise my head to look. My thoughts wandered, and I came near to sleeping, and afterwards I rubbed my eyes and lifted my head. The sun had all but gone down, and towards the bushes there was already darkness. I got up and brushed the dust from my behind and started to walk home again. In front of me, at the top of the incline, there was nothing coming but the dusk. I went into the house.

'Shellie – is you who come?'

'Yes, Ma.'

There was silence again, and emptiness, and the pain bore very heavily upon me.

After a little while, I said, 'What you doing? – lying down?'

She did not answer. I thought I'd go into the bedroom to keep her company.

As I entered, she was on her knees in front the bed, with clasped hands.

My eyes filled up again.

She whispered, 'You want us to say a little prayers together – for him?'

'Yes.'

I knelt down beside her.

10

Soon afterwards, I went to Cedar Grove with Mr Gidharee again. My mother had returned to work at the beach house and the days were so empty I was glad to go some place. I could have gone more often with Mr Gidharee if only Ma would let me. But she thought Mr Gidharee's kindness too much like charity, and she was a little embarrassed. Mr Gidharee was not like that at all, but she would not believe when I told her so. Anyway, on this day when I asked her she said, all right.

I listened for Mr Gidharee coming up the hill and I went out into the road to meet him. I had my cutlass and bag and I was dressed for the bush. I chased away the stray dogs that were making a racket, and I took the chain-leads of Lion, the brown dog, and Rover, the black-and-white.

When we had had a little peace from the strays and we were going on, Mr Gidharee said, 'When school open next week that mean we wouldn't go in the bush again, boy.' He said this as though he would be sorry.

'I mightn't be going back to school.'

He looked round sharply, 'Why not?'

'When Pa was here I had to stay home.'

'But he ain't here now.'

'I stay home two months already. In any case I have to start looking for work now.'

He said nothing, but I knew he was weighing up the situation. With our situation as it was, it could not have been hard to weigh up.

He said, 'How's your Pa?'

'We don't know yet. We ain't hear from Port-of-Spain yet.'

'Not *yet*?'

'Ma say if we don't hear by next week she'll send me up.'

'You ain't hear yet? Good God!'

I knew what he was thinking. The same thing had passed through my mind again and again. But the doctor here had said he was in touch with the Colonial Hospital and that if anything went wrong he'd let us know.

Mr Gidharee did not speak further. We walked up the hill and Rover was tugging me along and I was holding Lion, also, and Lion was walking with his nose to the ground and his tail curved over his back. They were both walking on the grass although the pitch was not yet hot from the sun. The grass was very wet with dew. I was just behind Mr Gidharee and I watched the strands of grey hair at the back of his head and I watched the way his hips jerked sharply with every step. He was wearing a blue-dock shirt and blue-dock pants, and he had that same broad belt round his waist, with his cutlass case hanging from it.

On Spring Flat he saw a car far away at the Spring Bridge end and he said, 'Tiger, mind you back-side!' All the other dogs were walking on the grass but Tiger was walking on the pitch. He did not have to speak to Tiger again, and this amazed me, and the car came up and passed.

'This Tiger does understand,' I said.

'They does understand, but you have to cuss them.'

I laughed.

At the moment both Lion and Rover were tugging me on, and I noticed Hitler was yelping. It was because we were nearing Cedar Grove that they were getting excited.

Once in Cedar Grove, we released the dogs and they fled up the road. Tiger, the spotted one, was in front, and Rover was behind him. They were both kicking up the red dust. Lion was running on the grass, with his nose to the ground, and every now and again he stopped, looked into the bush – his ear pricked up – then started running again. Hitler, the black one, just ran along coolly behind them. His tail seemed to curl right over, and his fur seemed a clean, glossy black from here.

'Hitler look like if he bathe,' I said.

'Ro always bathing them,' Mr Gidharee said.

In the distance I saw the dogs bolt into the track and disappear. The bushes on the roadside looked thicker and more tangled than I had known them and further in I could see the vines clasping the trunks of the big trees. There were little birds jumping about the bushes and their chirping filled the grove. There were *jeune males* and *via males* a-plenty and it crossed my mind I could bring my cage here and set sticky lagley gum and see what my luck was like. The truth was, I was almost fed up with catching birds now, but the sight of so many cage birds stirred me somewhat. There was also the screeching of parakeets in the trees and a flight of them swooped low across the road towards the river.

Mr Gidharee followed them with his eyes and watched them till they were out of sight. His brow was wrinkled and I knew he did not like the sight of them. He said nothing. We turned into the track.

After a moment he said, 'Well it look as if we'll have some rain, boy.'

'Think so?'

'Yes. Sure as day.'

Looking up now you could hardly see the sky. The bush edged in overhead, and even above this, the branches of the big trees kept out the sun. But it felt a great deal cooler, and it was almost dark here, through the track.

We went along, I, a little clumsy in my sandals, and every now and again Mr Gidharee looked back to see if I was keeping up with him. Then I saw the red boundary flowers before us, and the large clearing that was Mr Gidharee's place. Ahead was the big lazy river, and from there came the occasional yelping of the dogs.

We stood up where the track brought us into the rice field and Mr Gidharee was looking at the place. A great deal of the rice had been cut since I was last here, but there was still a lot more, and the rice far away to our left was only just ripening. He had reaped those that had been planted first and now he was working back to the newest part of the field. In the bare part – in front and to the right of us – he had forked up the ground and it was this he was looking at now.

'You cut a good bit already,' I said.

'Yes,' he said, as if his thoughts were far away, and then I heard him say: 'I wonder if this ground will take good sweet-potatoes.'

His face was all screwed up. It amused me. You could tell that planting was his passion. I could not suggest anything and I did not know if this ground would take sweet potatoes. At the other end of this field I had seen a lot of yams, and dasheens, and sweet and bitter casava, but I had seen no sweet-potatoes, and now I realised he had not given it a try yet. He rested a hand on his head then he was scratching his head, and he was very still for a moment. Then he looked round for me.

'You see that heap over there, Shell? Take this bag down there and empty it out and come and meet me by the shed.'

'Right.'

I walked over the bare piece of ground from which the rice had been gleaned. The heap he had shown me was near the very edge of the river. I trod on the prickly stalk-ends until I came to the part forked up. Then I walked over the hard, turned-up earth, towards the river bank. I came to the heap which turned out to be a lot of potato slips and I opened the bag and here was a lot more potato slips. As I bent to pour the slips out I started back with a cry, then I quickly composed myself. It was Hitler that had sprung out of the bushes beside me. 'Hitler! You – ' I stopped and looked to see if Mr Gidharee was by, then I said, 'You *bastard*!' He began wagging his tail. My heart was still thumping from the fright. 'You always doing that,' I said. 'You always doing this stupid thing!' He stood there wagging his tail and looking up at me.

The day-light had gone very dim and I looked up and there were lots of clouds in the sky and I could not even see where the sun was. The river before me eased by and was yellow-brown, and long grass from our side of the bank hung over onto it. I did not go too near to the edge for fear that crazy Hitler would push me over. The river looked rather wide and over on the other bank mangrove trees sent down huge roots into it.

I looked up at the sky again and then I turned away and there was Hitler sitting on his behind, waiting for me. I was no longer angry with him. 'Ah, Hitler boy, look like we'll have some rain, boy,' I said. He wagged his tail.

With Mr Gidharee I spent the morning planting potato slips and when it was twelve o'clock we stopped and went to the hut. We knew it was twelve by the sun being right overhead, and by the trees casting no shadows, and I knew it was twelve more so because of the rumbling noises my belly was making. Inside the hut there was a big cut calabash and Mr Gidharee took this and went outside. I went outside too and I watched him go down to the river's edge and fill the calabash with water and come back again. My face was greasy with sweat, and he said to me, 'You want to wash you face and thing? Go down there, by the water, and wash your face and hands man.'

Although I did not say anything, going down there and putting my hands into *that* water was the last thing in the world I wanted to do. This river was said to be infested with alligators, and everytime I looked at it there were alligators at the back of my mind. Mr Gidharee came back from inside the hut with two large sardine cans in his hand and he put them down and filled them with water. Tiger had been lying in the shade just beside the hut and as soon as he had seen Mr Gidharee go out with the calabash he had come and stood up right by the door and now Mr Gidharee had hardly filled the tins before he was lapping up thirstily. Mr Gidharee looked around him then he put two fingers to his mouth and whistled shrilly, and there was a racket in the bushes, and the next moment all three dogs, Lion, Hitler and Rover, were beside him. Right away Rover began lapping from the other tin. Lion stood on his hind legs trying to drink from the calabash, and Mr Gidharee said, 'Wait, Lion, you mad or what! You can't drink from the dam' calabash. Wait, like Hitler!'

Lion stood there wagging his tail, panting, his tongue hanging out.

When Tiger and Rover were finished, Mr Gidharee filled up the tins again and let the other two dogs drink. Then he put the calabash to his head and took a mouthful, and he shook the water from side to side in his mouth and spat it out. He put the calabash in the hut again and he said, 'Let's go and wash we hands and face.'

I walked behind him and we went to the river bank. He lay right over on his belly onto the grass and put both hands in the water and washed them, then he splashed water all over his face. 'Ah-h!' he said, 'cool and nice.' Then he rose from the ground and moved for me to do the same. I was very scared but I did not want him to see this. I glanced at him and luckily he was looking to see what the clouds were doing. So down I went, quickly, lay on my belly, hastily skimmed the water with my hands and passed my hands over my face, and got up. He was still looking at the cloud formation. Now he was shaking his head knowingly.

After a moment I said, 'The dogs does swim in this river?'

'Swim? Here? I don't even want them to drink this blasted water, far less swim. Especially in this part.'

'But why?'

'Why? Boy you dead or what! This place have alligators like peas!'

This made my blood creep. 'And you does still wash your hand here?'

'Why not? Who 'fraid alligator!'

I said nothing. My heart was thumping against my chest.

He said, 'I mean, the only thing is, those buggers could drown your dog like *that*.' He snapped his fingers.

I was looking at the brown water, half afraid that something would suddenly pop up. Mr Gidharee moved off and I hastily moved off after him and we walked back to the hut. Under the star-apple trees the low bush was red with bird pepper and Mr Gidharee picked some of them and put them into his pocket. The dogs were standing at the hut, waiting, for they knew they would soon get something to eat. There were four little bowls in the hut and Mr Gidharee unwrapped some half-cooked meat from a big leaf and he put chunks of it into the bowls for the dogs, then he put the bowls outside. I sat in the hut and I heard him outside saying, 'Now no blasted fighting today, eh!' When he came into the hut again he took out a big thermos flask from his knapsack and there was a big folded cloth and when he unfolded the cloth there was a lot of roti and dhalpourri for us to eat.

After dinner we worked quite hard, planting the sweet-potatoes in their beds – which were long loose mounds – and afterwards we planted pigeon peas. He showed me how to make the hole for the pigeon peas, and how to put them in. We put them in three to a hole, and every now and again he put in an ochro to give them shade in early growth. I never knew Mr Gidharee had so much land here, for we planted for a great length beside the river. The land was well-tended and this stretch was forked and very loose, with the soil itself dark brown and looking rich. When Mr Gidharee was working he did not talk much, but his hands were swift and his bottom was cocked in the air. We worked well into the afternoon and then I was sweating and he told me to go and sit down if I wanted, and he continued working. I went and leaned up against a tree, resting and looking at him and then I began looking at the river. Brown, lazy Ortoire slid by. The tide of the sea was in, for the river was flowing inland, towards deep forests. There were screeches coming from afar and they could be from the monkeys, or could be the parakeets. The sun was not brilliant now and it was definitely going to rain, for the sky was mottled wherever there were glimpses of it. Overhead the birds were making a riot in the trees. I looked towards the shed to see if I could spot the dogs, but there was only Hitler about. As I looked, Hitler pricked up his ears. I looked at Mr Gidharee again as he worked swiftly with his hoe and bag of dried peas. He worked very fast and yet he did not seem to be hurrying. After a while he put the hoe down and rose and straightened his back.

'How old you is now, Shell?' he said.

'Fifteen – going in sixteen.'

'Rosalie's just on fifteen,' he said.

There was a pleased look over his face. At the word 'Rosalie', I had shifted my eyes quickly and looked at the river. There was silence. Then Mr Gidharee bent down to his work again. I watched him and thought quite a bit until the evening came down and he stopped work.

11

A few days later my mother decided to send me to Port-of-Spain. The district doctor had no news for us and my mother wanted very badly to hear of my father. She was greatly overwrought by his being away and by her hearing nothing of him. All sorts of strange things were happening in the house these days and my mother took them as signs and portents. One night a door-clasp fell from a ledge onto the floor and my mother thought this to be a very decisive sign and she began to cry.

Now on this day she told me she would have to send me to the Colonial Hospital. It was the only way of our getting to know exactly what was going on. Telephoning was out of the question. This would be far too expensive and we could take all day without being connected. Even if we did have the money, and we tried, and got connected, the connection was sure to be to the wrong place. The telephone service was too inefficient.

I was to travel on the Friday. It would be wonderful to see my father again and to come home and report about him. I had never been to Port-of-Spain in my life but I knew I would be able to find the Colonial Hospital. I was very anxious to go.

Here on Pierre Hill, things were much changed. These days I had often gone to the cashew tree, but mostly there would be no one else about. When I had first met the boys it was August holiday time, but now, with September come, they were all back at school. Rosalie was back, too, and I hardly saw her, although I thought of her more than ever. I was not going back to school. In any case there was not much lost as I would have had to leave in a year's time, anyway. Lennard was due to finish at Christmas, and Joe, I imagined, would have another year of it. Joe's friend, the dull fellow, might have another year too. Like Joe, he wanted to be a motor mechanic. Rosalie Gidharee would have two more years – since she was just entering fifteen. I felt very lonely, seeing neither her nor the boys these days.

The cashews on the tree were now finished. Most of the thick, yellow-brown leaves were jagged or torn, and in places, sticks and stones had completely blasted away the ends of branches. When I came here now it was, oddly, for companionship sake.

Having so much time to myself – with my mother gone to work at the beach-house – I often thought of this place, Pierre Hill. Although I was not perfectly used to it yet, I liked it. There were coconut trees all around, though not quite as many as along the beach, and though we were supposed to be on a hill, just a little distance in front of our house mountainous land rose above us. Over there, it was green with low grass and with coconut trees, and there were houses at the top and along the side of the hill. Sometimes I stood in front of the house looking across at this, as there was nothing else to do.

Of course when school was dismissed in the afternoon the boys would be about again, but my mother would be at home, then, and would need me in the house.

Still, on Thursday evening I slipped down to the café at the foot of the hill. I was so excited about the journey to Port-of-Spain that I had wanted to tell Freddie about it. This café, I had come to realise, was Freddie's little place.

It was a pleasant-looking café, well stocked with rock-cakes and drops and buns in the glass cases, and with sweets and soft-drinks on the shelves, and there was a huge ice-box with an ice shaver on top of it, where Freddie probably made press, and snowballs, and maybe even ice-cream. When Freddie saw me his face lit up with surprise.

He said, 'Long time no see. I thought you left Pierre Hill, man.'

'Not yet.'

I leaned against the counter. There were two or three people sitting on benches against the wall. There was a small boy drinking snowball and blowing it every now and again, and this made me chuckle to myself.

I said, 'Freddie, you have a major little café here, you know.'

He had seen me looking around and he had paused to let me admire the place, and now as I had said he had a major café he looked very gratified and he cast his eyes around to see how nice it was. Then he said, 'not too bad.' He squinted, and shook his head, meaning the place was nothing much. I liked the look of the place.

'So Shellie, where you was all this time?'

'Oh, just home.'

'Home? So what – you young fellers don't go to school or what?'

'You know, I ain't going back – well – '

He looked puzzled. 'You is sixteen already? You ain't sixteen yet.'

'No, it's because of the old man.'

'Oh yes – Lennard was telling me about your old man in hospital or something.'

I was surprised. 'How come he know that?' I said, 'I ain't seen him for ages.'

I think he get that from the *dougla* girl.'

'Oh.'

I was very pleased that he had known. Of course it was clear Rosalie would have told them, but I had not thought of it until now.

I said, 'I ain't see those boys for weeks.'

69

'Oh, well, school open again, you see. Those fellers does go to school.'

He left me to attend to somebody and meanwhile I had another good look around the place. A picture over the ice-box caught my attention. When Freddie came back I said, 'Going to Port-of-Spain tomorrow.'

'Oh yes?'

'The old lady sending me up to see him.'

'I hope he's all right,' Freddie said. He looked so sad, as though he wished he could do something. He thought a little and then he said again, 'Boy, sickness is a hell of a thing, yes. I hope he wouldn't be too bad.'

'I hope.'

'Which way you going, through Rio Claro or through Sangre Grande?'

I had not thought of this before. My heart began to race a little, for the name 'Sangre Grande' sent Joan rushing into my head. I had almost forgotten about her. I thought it would be great to see her again. If I turned up in Sangre Grande she might be flabbergasted to see me.

I said, 'I think I'll go through Sangre Grande.'

Freddie left me to serve a few people who had just come in. I thought of asking him if he knew Joan and had any idea where in Sangre Grande she lived, but then I changed my mind because he and I were not all that friendly. He might not think me *discreet*. I almost chuckled. The next idea that came to mind was the idea of seeing Lennard. He knew a lot about Joan and since he had been encouraging me on at the dance perhaps he would tell me. Freddie came back, and I said, 'I'll try a snowball, Fred. Let me see if you could make snowball.'

He was amused at that. I was pleased too. I felt that at least I had to buy something in Freddie's café. I looked round at him as he shaved the ice.

Two of the people that had been sitting on the bench were still there, but the little boy was gone. The little boy who had been blowing the ice-cream. This nearly made me laugh out. It was odd how being here had lifted my spirit. Or perhaps it was just thinking about Joan. She had brightened the Discovery Day fair, and somehow she brightened me now.

Freddie finished the snowball and it had a lot of condensed milk and red syrup on it. It looked nice.

'This looking nice, Fred.'

'That's a special,' he said, humbly.

'Thanks, boy. This is a major snowball.' I pushed the money over the counter to him.

'What's this for?'

I understood what he meant but I pretended not to. 'No, this is for the snowball, I mean to say – '

'Don't be silly,' he said, pushing the money back.

'I mean – '

'Don't make joke,' he said, 'put that silver in your pocket.'

'Oh gosh, thanks a lot.'

'Thanks for what? Good Christ, this is something too?'

'Thanks, Freddie boy.'

'What time you travelling tomorrow?'

'First bus – I want to.'

'You'll have to get up real early.'

'I'll get up. I does get up all right – when I *have* to. I does wake up just like that. By the way, you know where Lennard house is?'

'Straight across the savannah. That house right behind the Foresters' Lodge.'

The road forked just at the foot of Pierre Hill, and there was a savannah spreading out from the right hand road. I thought of it now, and I knew the Foresters' Lodge, but I had never guessed Lennard lived there. It was a shame, I had been on

Pierre Hill so long and I hardly knew anything. I said to Freddie, 'Lennard is a man I want to see. I'll take a walk across there.'

'Don't forget, straight across the savannah like that.' He put both his hands out to show me how straight. 'Like this,' he said, 'and it's the one behind here.'

'Righto.'

After finishing my snowball I looked round at the café again and then I said cheerio to Freddie, and left.

12

Early the next morning I was up and away. The bus sped down the station hill, turning away from the Government School and into Manzanilla Road. For miles this was a straight flat road with palms on either side, and between palm-trunks and leaves, on our right, there was the rising sun, and, on occasions, glimpses of the sea. I was excited for the travelling and for the prospect of seeing Joan in Sangre Grande, but more so there was the excitement of seeing my father soon. I thought I'd go up to Port-of-Spain first and see him and on my way back I'd stop at Sangre Grande. Lennard had told me how to find Joan. He was very excited that I was going to Port-of-Spain. He said I must stop off and see Joan. Joan had written to him and asked about me. She had especially asked to be remembered to me. (For all I knew, Lennard was fibbing.) Anyway, he said I must go, then let him know if I saw her.

The road had now wound towards the beach, and here we were speeding along with the waves washing the shore close to us, and with the beach-sands silvery and broad, and with the palms seeming to crowd in upon us. Then after some miles we came to a sign saying 'North Manzanilla', and there was a road junction, and the bus turned inland into hilly roads flanked by forest trees. About half-an-hour later we rolled into the Cunapo Road, and here was Sangre Grande.

In the early morning Sangre Grande town was a hive of activity. Cars and carts and buses cluttered the streets, and bicycles, with their bells ringing, threaded precariously through the traffic. Crowds were jamming the pavements and the shops.

I was taken aback at the sight of such crowds, and at the traffic, and at the hugeness of the shops and stores that lined the main street. It was about eight o'clock now and the cafés were just opening, and in front of some of the shops vendors were setting up little stalls. The bus went past these places until it came to the terminal beside a railway station. Then it turned round and came to a stop, facing the other way.

I got out now and I had to catch one of the buses for Port-of-Spain. Stepping onto the ground I felt a thrill just from being in this place. The day had become rapidly bright and there was sun on the pitch now and on the houses. Over the tops of the houses, towards the way I had come, sunlight lit up thick forests. On the other side – towards Port-of-Spain – houses stretched far into the haze. It seemed as if the real, civilised world began from this town.

It was some time before I could cross the road and then I went to the bus stand and waited. I was thinking quietly of Gilt Street. This was Joan's street. Lennard had said it was close to the Police Station, just off the Cunapo Road. I was on the Cunapo Road now but I did not see the Police Station and no doubt it was somewhere close by, looking at me. This was always the case. I did not worry about Gilt Street because I knew I could find it when I got back.

As I waited for the bus to come I slowly grew possessed by

the thoughts of Joan. Joan meant Sangre Grande to me and Sangre Grande meant Joan. I kept thinking of her as she had been on Discovery Day. I was seeing her exactly as she looked then, with the ribbon in her hair, and with the blue silky dress – with the waist pulled in tightly because she was fat. She was not fat, really, but a little plump, and girls were always trying to make their waists look as slim as possible. I remembered her just as I had seen her first, with that waist-band pulled tight, and her smiling eyes and her soft-looking fatty cheeks. I remembered how I spun her, while dancing, and how she moved so lightly, and how she said, 'And you said you couldn't rhumba!' and how I was so thrilled that I was embarrassed. I was all filled up with her when the bus for Port-of-Spain roused me.

After this, there was the long wide road to Arima, and the long busy road to Curepe. My thoughts had dropped Joan now and I was thinking of my father. The nearer I got to Port-of-Spain it was the more I thought of him, and when I reached San Juan, and saw there were only a few more miles to go, my mind became excited and aflame. I sat with my heart thumping, while the great strange city slid into us.

13

The busy maze that was Port-of-Spain burst upon me. I knew I should never find the Colonial Hospital in this din without asking about a thousand times, so I thought the best thing to do was to take Lennard's advice and go to it by taxi. The noise of engines and car-horns, and the cries of people in the street had me quite dazed. The bus terminal was on Henry Street and I got out here and there was a taxi-stand not too far away. Most of the taxis were San Fernando bound, but there was one doing the town, and I went in. Pretending to be composed, I said, 'Colonial Hospital.' The driver said nothing but fixed his cap on his head, then he pulled out from the row of parked taxis and we joined the stream of vehicles going up the street.

I was craning my neck looking outside, for this was Port-of-Spain. All through one's life one heard of Port-of-Spain and now here it was, just outside. Port-of-Spain was a maze of colours and big buildings and street-signs, and of squares and promenades, and of noisy, teeming pavements. I sat back after a little while, dizzy, and I watched the driver sitting there in front of me. I was looking at the back of his head. His cap was at an angle, and he kept his head very straight, and he had not said a word to me yet. I looked at the dashboard, then over the dashboard and then all of a sudden our eyes met in his driving mirror. I glanced away and as I began looking out into the street again, the car stopped beside iron railings.

'Colonial Hospital,' the driver said.

Seeing that I was fumbling with the door he turned round, put his hand into my section, and opened the door. I got out and paid the fare. Then I stood up on the pavement and watched him drive off.

I had never before been in any building as vast as the Colonial Hospital, and it must have taken me at least half-an-hour – after seeing about a dozen people – to get to my father's bedside. This was not visiting time, and had not my father been very ill, and had I not come from so far away, the Ward Sister would have never allowed me to see him. That morning they had tapped him – which meant that they had drawn fluid from his inside – and he was so exhausted he was asleep. I stood at his bed and looked down on his face. He looked quite strange and quite ill, and they had the sheet drawn half-way over him. I felt for his hand under the sheet and there were tears welling up inside me.

He was not snoring but he was blowing rather heavily. His pyjamas were hospital pyjamas with the broad, sickly-red stripes, and there were big spotty stains all over them. The top button of the jacket was undone and I could see his chest, hairy, but with the skin looking flabbier than I had known it. There was a locker just beside the bed with an empty fruit bowl upon it, and in a recess provided to put things in, there was a bed-pan and one of those bottles for him to ease his bladder in. The place reeked of a lysol-lotion smell, which seemed to mix with a faint, depressing flesh-smell. I told myself I must remember to get some bananas for his fruit-bowl before going away. I looked at his face again and there was a nurse passing by who kept glancing across at me. There were a lot of very ill patients in the ward who seemed too weak to say anything, but they turned their heads my way. The nurse passed again – quite near to me – and she looked across at me but she did not say whether I should wake him or let him sleep. If she thought I would go away to Mayaro again without my father seeing me she was making a big mistake! The locker had a projecting piece, like a seat, which I guessed was exactly what it was, and since nobody told me to sit down, I sat down. My face was just next to my father's now. I said, 'Pa.'

I had said it quietly, but it reached him and he slowly opened his eyes. He turned his head on the side and he saw me and at once his eyes brightened and it was as if he could not believe. He said, 'Shell?'

'Yes – it's me!'

He tried to turn on his side but he could not, and he said, 'Turn me on the side.'

I looked round and sure enough the nurse was standing there

watching. Now she came up and she said, 'What's the matter, now, Mr Lammy?'

'Turn me on the side, nurse. Me boy come.'

'You was only tapped this morning,' she said. 'You lie down quiet and behave. You could talk without turning round.' She went away again.

'All right, nurse,' my father said.

My chest heaved. I looked round at the nurse as she went. I said, 'Who *she* telling to behave! Who she think she is?

'Is all right,' my father said, tiredly, 'that is their way. They don't mean nothing.'

I gradually calmed down about the nurse. I stood so Pa could see me better for he had to watch from the corner of his eyes. I looked down on him and I smoothed back the hair on his forehead and I said, 'You all right, Pa?'

'Yes,' he said. 'Yes, boy. This is murder.'

'What about this tapping business?'

'Boy, this is murder. A whole bucket. Boy, me inside – me inside raw like anything.'

He could not get enough breath to say many words at a time, but I was used to that. I did not want to ask him how they did this tapping. The very thought of it made my blood creep. Why did this thing have to happen to people like Pa, I did not know. There were lots of people who deserved this sort of thing but nothing ever happened to them. My father was a good man but a whole bucket of fluid had gathered inside him.

'Pa, how you feeling, really?'

'Weak like hell'

I could see it. He was really very ill. I did not know if he realised I was in Port-of-Spain, although he was there and talking to me. Maybe he did not even think of it. He was looking at me now the same way he did when we were at home and I had gone to his bed to talk. He was breathing rather short.

I looked down at the sheet where his belly was and it was a relief to see his belly flat, like a normal man's, instead of bulging like a pumpkin. Yet I was not much cheered.

'When you think you'll be coming home?'

'Home?' he came back as if from far away. 'Oh. Home. Boy, this is murder, yes. I don't know.'

He was beginning to show a little more life. Apart from the moment when he had recognised me and his eyes had brightened he had slipped back into a sort of dreaminess. Now he moved his neck as though he wanted to be raised a bit and I looked round and did not see the nurse but I was still afraid to raise him.

Just put the pillow a little more under me,' he said.

'Lie down as how the nurse put you.'

He glanced at me and there was that old look of defiance in his face. I smiled.

'So you not lifting me up?'

'No.'

His lips parted in a smile. I felt filled up.

I looked at him lying with his head turned to one side. 'You never like to lie down as how people put you!'

'God dammit! You can't tell me how to lie down!'

'Well you stay just how you is, that's all.'

'Wait nuh! Who is my father, you or me?'

I burst out laughing at this, and when he realised what he had said he gave his usual 'hey-hey' laugh, and the next thing I knew was that the Ward Sister was behind me.

'What's going on here?' she said, 'Mr Lammy, what's going on here? You realise what this place is?'

My father was cowed for a while and then he said, 'Me boy come to see me.'

'I thought you was a sick man,' the Sister said, 'I was under the impression you was only tapped this morning. Just hear that breathing of yours! And anyway you can't laugh out like that here. This is not visiting hour, you know.'

'All right, Sister,' Pa said.

She looked at me and I was very fearful she would ask me to leave but she did not bother. She lifted about three layers of sheets which had covered Pa's belly, and I had a glimpse of all the dressing and somehow the sight of it seemed to freeze up my inside. Through the cotton-wool and lint, blood had oozed right up to the bandaging. The Sister replaced the sheets and went away again.

Having seen under the sheets I fell silent, but Pa glanced across at me. 'How home, how your Ma. She all right?'

'Yes.'

'Good.'

'I mean, you know how Ma does worry.'

'Yes,' he said. 'I don't know what to say.' He looked very depressed.

'Well, she must worry. After all, not a word from this hospital. We didn't know if you dead or what.'

'They can't kill me so easy,' he said, and there was that smile again round his lips.

My spirits rose to see him cheerful. I saw he was going to speak so I waited.

'And talking 'bout writing – you think – you think this hospital does write to anybody? A man dead here – three weeks – only yesterday the family know. They came to see him.'

'Oh God!'

'You think they does – let you family know?' he said. 'Not them.'

I was silent. I wanted to let him get back his breathing properly, for he was beginning to look exhausted. Also, I was thinking of that family who came and heard the man was dead three weeks. Christ! I thought.

'But they – can't kill me so easy,' my father said.

Everytime I turned round now the nurse in the ward was looking at me and a while ago she had been talking with the Ward Sister, and now she had a trolley with shining little instruments. She had brought this trolley and left it in the middle of the ward and had gone back. I had a quick glance at the trolley, and I could see things like tiny barrels with long needles sticking out of them, and also little boxes, and little bottles, some with red liquid inside, and there was a great deal of cotton-wool. The nurse was out again presently. When she pushed the trolley the things made quite a clatter, and my father, without even looking, said, 'Injections.'

Oh God! I thought. It was not only the thought of injections that troubled me, but I knew I would have to go now. No wonder they were looking at me like that.

I looked back at Pa. A sudden brightness swept over his face, and he said, 'How little Gidharee?'

'Who?'

'Don't ask me who! The little *dougla*. What you mean "who"!'

I was laughing. 'Look Pa, I only see the girl once or twice, yes.'

'Once or twice?' he said, looking puzzled. He was trying to turn his face more towards me. The corners of his eyes found mine. 'You ain't so dam' slack, boy.'

I said nothing.

'I mean if you like a girl, don't feel shame for that. Listen, boy, I is you father and I'll tell you something. That little Gidharee girl have a pleasant little face and she look as if she have nice ways, so if you like her, boy, nothing to shame for in that.'

For once, in talking about Rosalie he did not seem to be

joking. I was a little surprised. I was going to say something when I heard footsteps, and here was the nurse.

She came right up to me and stood up and she looked at me and said: 'Well, you'll have to come again, young man.'

'Yes. Thanks, nurse. Thanks a lot. Going now.'

'Take your time. No hurry.'

But she stood there waiting for me to go.

After I took leave of my father I walked through many dark corridors to the blinding light of the street. I was not very depressed at the moment, though once, through the corridors, I nearly burst into tears. It was very painful, after seeing him, to leave him and go away. But he was very ill and if this great Colonial Hospital in Port-of-Spain was not the best place for him, where was? Somehow I felt hopeful that they'd do something for him here. He had been tapped so often and the fluid had gathered again, but I did not know what made me think that this time they would really cure him. Maybe it was just the Sister and her way that made me feel this. She did not look unkind, but severe. She gave me the impression that no nonsense could flourish about her. When she had lifted the sheets from my father's belly and had exposed all the bandaged wounds she had looked as though she meant no foolishness would be tolerated in that ward.

Out in the street I decided to walk to the bus depot and I had to ask my way. I walked along the teeming pavement, and the road was filled with vehicles and traffic lights, while huge concrete buildings seemed to crowd in to each other around one. At Henry Street there was the bus depot. The sun was very hot, and in the crowd the heat was unbearable. I was lucky because a bus was about to leave.

I got into it quickly and here it was cool, and I was glad to be out from the sun. Sitting here, there was the glare outside, and

81

there was the steady drone of the town, and the tooting of car horns, and now there was the sound and vibration of the bus engine and we were ready to pull out. Suddenly my thoughts were in the hospital ward. The bus pulled out and I felt a great pang within.

14

Back in Sangre Grande, I had no difficulty in finding Gilt Street. Joan had a shock from not expecting someone like me to turn up, and I spent a most enjoyable afternoon at her home. I had caught her at home during her lunch time and her mother said she could stay at home if she wanted. She had a younger sister, Charmayne, and she had told her mother and Charmayne about the Discovery Day fair, and about how I was drinking, and they made great fun about it. The mother asked had I had lunch, and I said yes, but Joan insisted that I had not. So the mother gave me lunch. While I was eating, Charmayne was ready to leave for school and she came and shook my hand and said cheerio. Charmayne was about twelve and she was very shy and as she shook hands she had her school-books half covering her face.

After Charmayne left, the mother went out to the backyard to do some washing and Joan sat and talked to me a little. There was a little brother, Jake, playing about on the floor, and I was watching him. Joan and I talked about Mayaro and about lots of other things, and I kept on thinking how grown she had become since last Discovery Day. After a while she left me to go and change her school-clothes.

When she came out again I said, 'Girl, your mother doesn't mind you talking with boys?'

I had been thinking about her mother somewhat. If you talked to girls, mothers always thought there was something in it. Her mother looked very pleasant but I was a bit uneasy.

'It depends,' Joan said.

'How you mean?'

'Well, in your case, it's as if she knows you, you see, because she knows all about you. But on the whole she's all right. Mind you, she doesn't stand for any low-dodges.'

'And you don't go in for low-dodges.'

'Sometimes,' she giggled.

'What sort?'

'Little things in the house. Oh, I don't get into any scrapes with boys – if that's what you mean.'

'What you really told them about me?'

'Oh, about Discovery Day and so on. About how you was tipsy and thing, and how Lennard and this Gidharee girl had to carry you home.'

I laughed. 'What they said?'

'They laughed.'

'I didn't know you knew I was tipsy.'

'You wasn't tipsy, you was drunk as a fish.'

I laughed out so hard I had to put my hands to my mouth quickly, remembering her mother outside.

'So your mother doesn't mind you having boy-friends?'

She gave me a sideways look, 'What you trying to find out?'

'If you have any boy-friend,' I said boldly.

'The answer is "yes."' She was laughing and looking away.

'All right,' I said quietly.

I felt something brush against my foot and I looked down. I had completely forgotten baby Jake. He was on the floor beside me and there was a large flat book by his side and he was playing with a toy lorry which had rolled under my chair. I bent and picked up the book. I had suddenly grown cold with Joan – because she had a boy-friend – but then I realised how silly I was, and I tried to be easy again and I said, 'You know I was thinking of going for some sweets for Jake?'

'Oh, Jake's all right,' she said. 'Perhaps later, eh?'

At the word 'sweets' Jake looked up. I laughed. He laughed too. I could hardly stop laughing.

I started looking through the book and it was all about two Portuguese children from Brazil. There were nice pictures in the book, and these Brazilian children were visiting North America, and wherever they went there were pictures to show. The children were José and Rosita, and the book called them 'Zay and Zita, our Portuguese friends.' This amused me. They were like very real friends in the book and were up to all kinds of mischief in North America, but whenever they did something wonderful, they were 'Zay and Zita, our Portuguese friends'.

'This is a nice little book,' I said to Joan.

'You mean old Zay and Zita.'

'I like it,' I said, 'I mean, I like this sort of thing.'

I looked at the book again, getting absorbed in it, and then I said, 'Well, I'd better go now, then. Perhaps you have things to do.'

'Things to do? What's wrong with you? I should be at school now, boy, and I only stayed home because you here. Don't tell me you leaving already.'

'Okay.'

'I mean if you feeling bored here perhaps we could go out a bit. Just a minute.'

She took up baby Jake and went outside. After a little while she came in again. 'You want to go for a little walk – see Sangre Grande a little?'

'Oh, yes. Yes, please.'

'Just a second.'

As she was going into the other room, I said, 'Your mother still washing?'

'Yes.'

'She remind me so much of my father.'

And then I remembered that I had not even told Joan that my father was ill and that I had just come from seeing him at the hospital in Port-of-Spain. Now there was the sharp pain of remembering him, and of the Ward Sister raising the sheets and showing his bandaged belly. I sat there, but was again in the Colonial Hospital, and I was only brought back by Joan's appearing again. Jake was tidied up and he looked very smart. He was wearing a *Junior Commando* jersey.

'Come, Jake,' I said.

'Go to uncle,' Joan said.

This made me smile a little.

'Something wrong, Shellie?'

'No. Why?'

'You look so depressed.'

'Oh, no,' I said.

'You ready to go for the walk?'

'Aha.'

'Let's go then.'

Out in the town I was very excited walking beside Joan, with people seeing us and thinking she was my girl. They probably thought she was my wife and that little Jake was my son. It was quite outrageous to think like this, for I was only fifteen, and Joan, despite her looking so grown up in this dress and in Cuban-heeled shoes, could hardly be older than that.

'How old you is now, Joan?'

'Going in sixteen.'

85

'Oh, yes? That's funny. Same here.'

We were walking very slowly because of Jake, and stealthily I was having a thorough look at her.

All of a sudden she looked round and said: 'Shellie, why you really come to Sangre Grande, talk the truth.'

'To see somebody I like.'

'Well you shouldn't do that.'

'Why not?'

'Well I mean I have my boy-friend and all that.'

'That's nothing. That's all right.' I looked at her and laughed but she was not joking now. She was taking me quite seriously. I was growing to take her seriously too, but at the moment I was only having a game with her.

'Girl, if you know how I was thinking about you after that Discovery fair!'

'But why?'

'Especially how we was dancing and thing.'

'And what's dancing. You better think about *Rosalie Gidharee*.'

'We ain't in nothing.'

She was quiet.

'Who told you about me and Rosalie anyway?'

'Don't worry. I was up there, and I have two eyes in my head,'

'What you talking about?'

'I know what I'm talking about all right.'

'Okay, believe what you want.'

'Naturally.'

I had grown quite irritated with her. I could not stand this for long. There is a time for everything, but not with girls!

And yet, as we walked on, she was so pretty to look at that I kept glancing across at her. As she walked, half-bent, holding

Jake's hand, I noticed how developed she had become in the few months since Discovery.

It was August then and now it was November. Then, there were no straps at her back. But I could see straps now through her organza dress. Thinking of her, I said to myself, 'You know what – I love you bad; and I'll have to get you!' But I walked on as if I was merely thinking of the weather. When we got to the junction by the Police Station Jake would not walk any more and Joan had to carry him because he would not come to me. I said, 'Come to Uncle,' and I looked at Joan's face but there was only a forced smile. Cars, bicycles, and buses were rushing by in the street. There was a long silence between us two, and finally Joan said, 'How you liking Sangre Grande?'

'This is a nice place. This is a major place, girl.'

'It's quite nice,' she said.

This bit of talk seemed to break the tension and soon we were easy again. However, after a great deal more walking about in the hot sun I was beginning to have enough of Sangre Grande. But I did not want to show I was already fed-up. But soon I could not take it any more and when I saw that Joan did not mean to stop, I said, 'You tired, Joan?'

She saw the point right away. 'Oh, I see. I think I know who's tired,' she said, laughing. 'Anyway, if you want to go back, okay.'

'Yes, man, Joan. This sun is punishment.'

She was much amused. 'Hear him! Okay, let's go back.'

Soon after we returned Charmayne was back from school. I did not delay much longer but started to say good-bye. I shook hands, but I did not make any fuss about Joan, for she had let me squeeze her hand under the table while I was talking to her mother. So things had gone suddenly bright for me. As I was going down the steps now. I thought of Jake. He was sleeping.

Christ, I thought, I didn't buy Jake those sweets! I said good-bye again and they answered, good-bye, almost in chorus. The father was still at work and there was a big brother, Alan. They regretted that the father and Alan did not see me. I did not mind too much. I never liked girls' fathers or big brothers. Anyway, I was soon out into the street.

15

It was heading hard for the end of the year when my father came home again, and I was so pleased. I was just returning from the Post Office when I saw him walking up the hill in front of me. There was no mistaking him with the deer-brown jacket and the slightly leaning walk. I felt so filled-up and liquid inside, I could not run to meet him.

I came upon him as he was opening the door of the house. He looked back and he saw me. 'Shell,' he said, his face lighting up. My eyes began to run like a river.

'What you crying for,' he said.

I could not answer.

'You have no cause for that. Look how you getting to be a big man.

I was beside him now and he put his arm about my neck and we went inside. He sat on the settee a little breathless. Walking up the hill always took the wind out of him. I took off his jacket and hung it up. I wiped my face with my sleeves but I was not composed yet and tears were still sliding down my face.

He did not say anything and I supposed he was giving me a chance to compose myself. I was sitting beside him and he still had his arm about me. I was conscious of his slightly rasping breath and this troubled me a little as I had expected the asthma was gone. I looked at him sideways, and his eyes were taking in the room. The place was tidy and shining clean, as though we had been expecting him. But this was the way my mother always left the place before going to work. He looked around and I could see his heart was pleased. After a while he turned to me: 'Your mother at the beach-house?'

'Yes.'

'Go down and tell her the boss come home.'

This cheerfulness made me almost all right again.

He said, 'How's everything, boy. How you going?'

'Okay.' I hesitated a little and then I said, 'Doing a little work – picking cocoa.'

Directly I could see this upset him. He had had it as his ambition that I must not do labouring work. He was such a sick man but he was still very proud and I could see that he was hurt. I wanted to pass this off so I said, 'And what about you – how you travel down?'

'Not too bad.'

There was a little silence. As I looked at him from the side I noticed his belly was not heavy and I hoped to God this was all right now and they would not have to tap him any more.

He said, 'So you didn't try to get the job in Port-of-Spain again?'

'Pa, that is hopeless.'

'Well, what sort of ambition you have, to go and work picking cocoa!'

I said nothing.

'You used to say you want to be all sort of big things – lawyer, doctor, big profession. That is how you'll be a lawyer? – working in the cocoa-field?'

'I *know*, Pa,' was all I could say. He ought to have realised that my having said I would be a lawyer, or a doctor, was just wishful thinking. At least you had to have education and go to some college or something to be any of those things. It used to please him to hear me say big things like what I'd be but he ought to have known better. There was only one solicitor in the whole of Mayaro and that was Inness. Inness, the big-wig. In any case, in this house it was a job to get enough to eat and drink and wear, let alone to afford to go to college. And Pa himself was in no position to help. Having left school I could not sit around doing nothing. I had to take the first thing that came along. I glanced at him now and he still looked distressed. The heaving of his chest was distinct.

'Pa, don't worry. O God, you just come from *hospital*!'

'I just come from hospital,' he said, 'and I have to go back. And my days as good as finished. But I don't want you to be a bleddy *good-for-nothing*!' He said this very bitterly, hitting the bed with his fist.

'You have to go back?' I was dismayed. 'I mean I didn't know you had to go back.'

He did not answer. He was still cross about my job.

I said, 'Besides I don't have to be a *good-for-nothing* because of picking cocoa.'

'What is cocoa-picking? Nobody does have to have brains for that. Why you don't look for something where it have to have brains!'

'How? You tell me how to get a job like that.'

He did not say anything for a moment, and then he said, 'You is a boy who have brains. You have it and I know you have it. If it wasn't for this sickness, by Christ, you wouldn't be in that damn cocoa.'

'But what you worrying out yourself for? Look how you blowing.'

He was quite worked-up. Now he shook his head.

I said, 'Sometimes I can't understand you. I ain't in any trouble. I ain't kill nobody. No wonder you always going back to hospital. What you have to go back again this time for?'

He was still sullen and didn't want to say anything, and then he mumbled, 'They only let me out for Christmas.'

'Only for Christmas? So what is all this time you spend there for? You mean to say they can't get you better or something?'

'Boy, it's like hell, to tell you the truth. I wouldn't hide nothing from you.'

As he turned to me I noticed the same old heaviness under his eyes – only a little slighter than usual – and I felt cheated and hurt.

'So you mean the fluid still gathering.'

'They can't stop it.'

'Christ!' Despair swept on me like a storm. 'Pa you mean to say in that big Colonial Hospital they can't do nothing?'

'And on top of that, I mustn't eat this, I mustn't eat that. All the nice things I like – coo-coo and thing – I can't eat. I don't know how the hell they expect – they expect me to live.'

As he had talked so much he looked quite weary now, and he had to stop in each sentence to catch his breath.

His was the face of a cornered bull. For myself, I knew that until the bitter end I would hope. Even against hope. As I looked at him now and I could see under the brave face how frail he was and yet how much a man.

I thought of the big hospital and the many weeks he had spent there and I said, half to myself, 'You no bl – ' and I stopped suddenly.

'What?'

'You no better off than before you went.' I was about to say, You no blasted better off, when I caught myself.

'But I'm still there, fighting,' he said.

'What about the specialist feller in San Fernando?'

91

'You crazy or what? I could pay any specialist?'

'And you don't want me to work in the cocoa! Look, if they can't cure you up there we'll have to do something. We'll have to find the money somehow and see that specialist?'

'Nobody will ever cure me,' he said, 'and this is from good quarters.'

He had turned to me slowly. Now he said, 'Stop that!'

I held my head in my hands.

'Big man like you. Every two, three minutes you eyes full with water.'

'Pa, I'm not.'

'You is a man or woman, for God's sake!'

I said nothing. As I lifted my head tears were dripping from my chin.

This must have softened him, for he said now: 'You think anybody could kill me?'

'You just said they'll never cure you!'

'Well you bother with what I say. What you think they have Doctor Pierre and all those surgeons up in San Fernando for.'

'You only saying that to make me feel nice.'

'Look, you see how flat me belly is?'

'You only trying to sweeten me. They'll tap you again.'

When he saw I would not be content he said, 'Boy, look here, life hard, but we can't give up, eh?'

'We mustn't give up.'

'And you sticking with you old man?'

'But you know that. You know I'll never give up when it comes to that – I mean, you know that.'

'Sometimes I does like to hear you talk. You does talk like a real man. You is a *wall*.'

'You, too. I take after you.'

'You is a *stone-wall*,' he said.

A few minutes afterwards I left to go to the Ocean Star beach-house to tell my mother that Pa had come. She came back with me right away. She was so happy and moved that even before she got home her face was wet with tears. We were the same in this sort of thing. I took after her in this. When we got back I stayed in the road while she went into the house. I did not want to see her breaking down for joy. I thought I'd give them a little time before I went in.

As I was standing in the road looking in the direction of the cashew tree and towards the shops, Rosalie Gidharee came out of the gap in their fence and walked out into the road. She saw me and she waved, and I waved back. She stood up looking towards me, seeming to want me to walk down to her. I stood there and she ambled very slowly towards me on the other side of the road, and when she got to the cashew tree she stopped. I turned away, pretending to be looking at the houses on the hill, but as I glanced back and my eyes caught hers she beckoned to me. I reluctantly walked down towards the cashew tree, thinking the while of what I'd say to her, and when I got there I said, 'Listen Rosie, Pa come. I can't stay out here now.'

She was excited. 'Your Pa come? Really? And you didn't say a thing!'

'He only just come. Just a while ago. Have to go in. See you.'

'Okay then. I could imagine how glad you is.'

'But he have to go back, you know.'

'Oh shocks!'

'Anyway, I'll see you, Ro. I'll tell you about it.'

'Okay, see you.'

'See you.'

I went back into our yard but not into the house yet. There was a clump of bushes between our house and the cashew tree and so Rosalie could not have seen me standing up here. I stood up near the steps and I wondered about her, and I wondered if when I saw her again I should tell her about my girl-friend,

Joan. Life was so strange, and girls so hard to understand. At the Discovery Fair I had wanted Rosalie so much and would have done anything to win her, but she had been to busy running after Joe to bother about me. But Joe did not care. Now that I had got a girl-friend she seemed to be running after me.

Of course there was no wavering in my mind regarding Joan and Rosalie. Since that day in Sangre Grande Joan had become everything to me. Having her, I no longer cared about any other girl.

I had not seen Joe for some time and I had heard he had gone away to learn to be a motor mechanic. I wondered what had developed between Rosalie and himself. The answer was bound to be: nothing. I thought maybe Rosalie had realised by now that he did not care. I wondered what made her turn to me all of a sudden. I did not mind this very much, but the friendlier she was to me, it was the nicer Mr Gidharee became, and now he was always asking me to go to Cedar Grove with him. He was the sort of person you couldn't help liking very much. Rosalie was nice, too, and pretty, and I had several times thought of making the most of her, but somehow I did not want to do this, for Mr Gidharee's sake. Also, I could not think of Joan and flirt with Rosalie. It was impossible, Whenever I thought of it something just went dead inside me.

I wondered if Rosalie had gone in yet. From in front the steps I walked stealthily back towards the road. There was a telephone pole over a drain on our side – barely in view of the cashew tree – and I went and stood up behind the pole and peeped towards the cashew tree. Quickly I pulled in my head behind the pole again. Rosalie was still standing there. Rover, the black-and-white dog, was with her now, frisking around her. My heart was thumping. When I had peeped she seemed to have been staring straight towards the telephone pole. I walked back into the yard and this time I went up the steps and into the house.

My mother was a long time getting over my father's arrival, and she was very strange all evening, and soft, and she looked as though she did not quite believe my father was here. She made supper early, and the day being so hot, she made lime-punch, and it was while we were having the lime-punch, with my mother washing-up in the kitchen, that I had my father alone for a while.

'Pa, you remember that little *dougla* girl?'

'You mean little Gidharee?'

'Aha.'

'Of course. Why? What happen?'

'Well it's like this. At first I used to like her, as you know, and she liked somebody else, and now I like somebody else, and you know the silly girl seem to be liking me.'

'Well what the hell I hearing here!'

'I know it sound funny but that's how it is.'

'Well let's hear you again – *You* like *she* and *she* like *you* and – '

'No,' I laughed. 'Not so. You see – '

As I began talking, my mother came in.

' – You see the cocoa pods just isn't – '

'Maybe witchbroom,' he said.

My mother looked at us and she went out into the kitchen again. I grinned at my father.

He said, 'If you think she ain't smart!'

'I know.'

'Now tell me about this Gidharee girl, quick.'

It was difficult to explain everything to him, for it was so mixed up, but I started telling him the story and he made something of it.

He said, 'I didn't know when you left me in hospital you went on the spree looking for girls.'

'I didn't go on any spree. This was a girl who was here on holiday and was in the Government School Discovery Day.'

'And who is this Lennard?'

'Lennard is a feller here in Mayaro. He and Joan is friends. But Joe and Rosalie used to be real friends.'

'You keep on saying "real friends". What you mean by "real friends"?'

'Boy-friend and girl-friend.'

'Well say that. And this Joe just gone like that. Just vanish. He's a mystery man or something?'

'Well he gone to Princes Town to learn motor mechanic. He just finish school this term. In any case he wasn't bothering with Rosalie.'

'And so she just take you up.'

'It look so.'

'Well boy, this Gidharee girl like you a long time now.'

'I don't know.'

'You don't know but I know. And this Joan – she way to hell up in Sangre Grande, I can't see how she could be your girl-friend.'

My mother came in at this stage and I had to keep the talk going so it wouldn't look suspicious, and I said, 'All the while it's dry, we could pick okay, but, you know, when it start to rain – ' and I stalled.

My mother looked at me. She did not seem to have anything more to do outside and she went into the bedroom. My father bent across to me and whispered, 'All right, don't mind. We'll talk tomorrow when she gone to work. Just mark the place. Okay?'

'Okay.'

16

The next day as soon as my mother had left for work and Pa was properly awake, and settled, and had his coffee, and after I had hidden his pipe, I raised the talk again at the point where we had left it off. As we were talking we heard the riot of the dogs in the road and I drew the curtains a little and we both leaned over to watch Mr Gidharee pass by. As Mr Gidharee reached level with our door I drew my head in and at the same time he looked our way and caught my father's face square in the curtains. He brought the dogs into our yard and there was the barking and baying of the other dogs.

'Ay, Mr Lammy,' he said.

Pa had now drawn open the curtains and opened the door properly, and he said, 'Ay, Mr Gidharee.'

'Rosalie tell me you here. How you feeling now?'

'Not too bad, thank you.'

'I really glad to see you, man. I mean we is neighbours but this is the first time we meet face to face.'

'Yes,' Pa said wistfully. 'You know how it is. All the time it's up and down to hospital.'

'In fact only yesterday the wife – only yesterday Marie was telling me. You say you feeling okay now?'

'Well not *okay*. I can't say that. But the way things going it's not too bad.'

'Well I hope so. For Shell sake, at least. Where Shell?'

'Look him here,' Pa said. I showed my face and smiled and Mr Gidharee smiled. Then he laughed, showing his brown teeth. 'This is a hell of a Shellie,' he said.

'Oh yes?' Pa said.

'I mean we does have a lot of jokes in that Cedar Grove.'

I stayed there, with my head beside Pa's and I couldn't help laughing to see Mr Gidharee laugh. Almost everything he did made me laugh.

Pa said, 'Well he's a boy like that. Thanks very much for the little things.'

'For what things?' Mr Gidharee pretended to be puzzled.

'For the little sweet cassava and peas, you know, and fruits, and all that. They does tell me everything. He come quite in Port-of-Spain to see me and he tell me all about that. Thanks very much.'

'Don't thank me, thank *God*,' Mr Gidharee said. He said it as a joke and they both laughed.

Mr Gidharee went on: 'No, I mean I know how you feel but that ain't nothing at all. We is neighbours and we have to help one another. I could do a lot more but you know how people does talk – you is a sick man and always in hospital and you have you wife alone here – you know how tongues does wag. I 'fraid to even tell you wife "morning" for what people might say. So I see Shellie and you know, he's a nice, quiet boy, and I know the position, so I say, boy, come with me and give me a hand in the garden and bring home a few things. So you see, it's not charity because he giving me a hand, too. I have lots and lots of things in that garden man, he could come and take and bring home whatever he like. That ain't nothing really, man. You know, he's a boy I like.'

'Thanks very much,' Pa said. 'You don't know how much I thank you.'

While Mr Gidharee was talking I was looking at the dogs. Rover, the black-and-white one, had been looking up at me all the time, and wagging his tail. Tiger was keeping his nose to the ground and following so many imaginary scents that he was completely entangling his leads with the leads of the other dogs, and while talking, Mr Gidharee was continually having to disentangle Tiger's lead. Hitler was standing up attentively, looking a little impatient, and Lion, the brown one, was lying down, his head resting on his front paws, red tongue outside.

These dogs had only just got a little peace. The strays, having bayed and barked themselves hoarse, had gone in again from the hot sun. From within the house I could see the sun bright on the pitch, and towards the lime tree in our yard the air looked shimmering. Above Mr Gidharee's head the sky was a dome of blue. This would be a scorching day.

Mr Gidharee and my father talked a little more and then Mr Gidharee said, 'Well okay papeeyo, I'd better go now. Think I'll loose these dogs. God it hot!'

He did not loose the dogs, however. As he went out into the road, there was the temporary mêlée of the strays again, but they soon got fed up, and Mr Gidharee walked up the road in peace. After he had gone we talked about him, and Pa said what a nice man he was. We talked about Rosalie again and Pa was all for my stringing along with her, because he liked Mr Gidharee so much.

'You and he is the same thing,' I said.

'He's a nice man. He'd be a father to you.'

'I have one father already. Besides, marrying Rosalie isn't marrying *him*.'

'And what's wrong with Rosalie?'

'Nothing,' I said calmly, 'she's all right.'

'Well what the hell!'

'But I love Joan.'

'You mean you *like* Joan.'

'What's the difference between like and love?'

'When you love somebody you love them to get married to them.'

'So when people love God they want to get married to Him?'

Pa laughed. He was thinking of a suitable reply, and then he said, 'God is not somebody.' I laughed at that, and then I got serious again and I said, 'So Pa, what if I *really* want to get married to Joan?'

'Listen, boy, you have plenty time for marrieding. You not even sixteen yet. You can't talk about marriage now.'

He stopped a little to catch his breath, then he said, 'I'll like to see you get married – to somebody nice. Before I close these eyes.'

'You wouldn't close those eyes now.'

'Hope not.'

'As I tell you already, I like Joan bad, and I think I'll like to get engaged to her.'

'Boy, you is a crazy boy, yes! You don't even *know* the girl. You only see her a few times. And before, you was so mad about this dam' Gidharee girl. You think writing letters to Sangre Grande every day is something? You don't even know what going on over there now. Go for what you could see, boy.'

'I like Joan and I *like* her, that's all. And she likes me. That's all I know.'

Pa looked a little resigned, and he said, almost to himself: 'And Gidharee so nice to him, yes. And appreciate him and everything. And this is no hand-to-mouth man, you know. This boy don't even know his own luck.'

I said nothing.

'How old Rosalie is now?'

'She is a year younger than me.'

'Well that's just nice. And you going for Joan.'

I kept an icy silence. I supposed he knew he could not change my mind. Sometimes I marvelled at my own stubbornness. Nothing could make me give up Joan.

I said, 'Look Pa, I know my mind. The only reason why I ask

you this is because Rosalie's nice and I like her a little and all that, and I know this Mr Gidharee playing smart – well not playing smart, but I know what happening, and I don't want to encourage anything.'

'Don't pull away from him, though, whatever happen – because he is a good man. And whatever happen, *don't get Rosalie in trouble.*'

I was silent at this point.

'You know what I mean?'

'No.'

'You is a big man, you know what I mean.'

'I know what you talking about.'

'If she ain't good enough to married to – in good time – she ain't good enough to play round with!'

'I know what you mean,' I said.

'And this Joan – if you so serious about her well have to see her some time.'

'That's another thing I wanted to talk to you about, Pa.'

'Shoot.'

'I wanted to bring Joan here. I mean to visit and thing.'

'But naturally.'

'But I ain't tell Ma yet. Ma don't know a thing about Joan.'

'Don't worry about that.'

'I mean, somehow I can't tell Ma about it. You know.'

'But you could tell me!'

'Well you so different.'

'How?'

'I don't know. I just don't feel no shame for you. I was even telling Joan that you is my father but I could tell you anything.'

'Every two words you say you have to bring in this Joan, Joan. We'll have to see this so-called Joan. I'll talk to your Ma.'

'Okay?'

'Leave things to me,' he said. 'Big man like you 'fraid to talk.'

'Okay, Pa.'

Sometimes Pa understood me better than I knew. When it came to talking about girls I was very, very distant from my mother. Perhaps this was the usual sort of thing, for boys. But I knew that the friendship between my father and myself wasn't common. Because I'd heard boys talk on these things. Some boys were terrified to let their fathers know they had girls. But my father used to tell me about girls from the time I was about eleven. He made life and love look so true and honest that it always made me wonder what people were so silly about. People were always whispering about love and about what happened and so on, but Pa spoke to me quite openly. Very many evenings we sat talking about school and if I talked about a particular girl a great deal he would know that I liked her and sometimes he'd tease me about it. But Joe said he couldn't mention girls in his house.

With my mother, though, there was never anything said on the subject. Whenever she told my father of the village goings-on, she acted so secretively, I was amazed. Most times I had known of these things even before she herself did, but even if I didn't know my father would tell me afterwards. This was the way he was, and this was why I liked him so strangely. Maybe there were other things too.

Now he was going to ask my mother if it was all right for Joan to visit. He was already keen on Joan, for my sake.

17

The next week was a fortnight to Chrismmas and the shops and stores seemed suddenly to wake to life. My father was still feeling well but it was clear that the fluid was gathering under his heart again. My mother and I were depressed about it but it had not been unexpected. The cheerfulness of my father made things faintly tolerable in the house.

I found no regular work, but at this busy Christmastime I was again picking cocoa on Gordon Grant's estate. It was very diverting to be in the heart of the cocoa plantation with the cocoa trees and immortelles forming a roof above and keeping out the fierce sun. It was semi-dark in the cocoa-field and the sharpness of green leaves and the yellow and red of the ripening pods made the place very strange. Also, underfoot, there would be the red, cockerel-shaped flowers of the immortelle tree.

We had long bamboo rods with cocoa-knives at the ends of them and all day long we went from tree to tree reaching for the cocoa-pod stems and stabbing at them or twisting them, letting the pods fall beneath the tree. Sometimes we broke a ripened pod and sucked the juice-coated cocoa seeds, with the rich, sharp tang of cocoa in our noses. At such times, taking a rest, we would sit down and talk to the women who were gathering the pods into heaps.

Yet, as a whole, the day would be very tiring, and towards evening, with the bushes full of the shrieks and whistles of forest creatures, my brain would begin to swim. With the flight of the first roosting parakeets – the wing-flapping, screeching parakeets – we would know that breaking-off time was near. Some of the men would begin chanting, 'It's Time For Man Go Home!' and not long after this the foreman would blow a whistle, and we would finish work.

This would be a great relief. If we were working near a stream I would then take a bath before going home – just to get the reeking cocoa-smell off me. And when I arrived home, usually my father would be sleeping, and though my mother might be in, I would feel quite desolate and alone, and if the sun had not quite sunken yet, I would go out and sit on the front steps. After the sun went down and the lamp was lit I would go and fetch my writing pad and sit at the table and write to Joan. I did this every night.

Mostly I wrote to Joan about the cocoa-field and about the Indian girl, Sonia. Sonia was the girl gathering the picked cocoa pods in our part of the field. I got to be very friendly with her and sometimes I shared her roti and dhal. This food was very tasty – hot, with a lot of pepper, and I liked her for it. Joan wrote to me that she would like to know what the france was going on between me and this Sonia so I'd better let her know at once.

Sometimes Sonia made me think.

One evening, after the whistle had gone, I went to take a bath in the stream. I took off all my clothes and went into the water for a swim. I was certain everybody had gone and at least I had made sure all the women had cleared out. I dived into the water and it was cool and refreshing and I swam about a little and then I began to wash myself. Suddenly I heard the crackle of broken brambles and when I looked round, there was Sonia! I dived into the deep part quickly, and stood up where the water was up to my chest.

Sonia was laughing: 'You shame for me? What you shame about? I only come back for me cocoa-rod.'

'Well take up your cocoa-rod and go!' I said.

'Well look at this little boy – talking to me like that.'

Cocoa-pickers were supposed to be superior to gatherers and I really felt like shouting at Sonia. I stood there in the water bewildered and embarrassed. I was embarrassed mainly because she was so much older than me. She was at least twenty. If she had been around my age I would not have felt such deep shame – in fact, it might have been the opposite. But this was different. I was so angry I did not know what to do.

'What you so shame for, boy?' she said. 'What you have to hide?' She was convulsed in laughter.

'You come back here just to *watch*!' I said in a temper.

'I come back to watch *you*? But hear this little boy?'

'You didn't come back for any cocoa-rod. You left any cocoa-rod here? Listen, Sonia, work finish, and I want to be private here.'

'So this is you bath-room?' She burst out laughing. She did not seem the slightest bit uncomfortable.

I stood there looking at her, with her looking at me, and it was a good thing the water was not clear and she could not see that part of me below it. Her large face was smiling. Her hair fell onto her shoulders, and she had a cloth over her head – an *orhoni* – and this came down to her left shoulder. On her feet were rubber sandals. Strangely enough, she looked like a madonna against the trees.

I was still very angry with her. I would have got out of the water and changed and gone home, leaving her standing right there, had I not been naked. I said to her, 'Okay, let's see how long you'll stay here. I could stay here whole day and whole night. Tomorrow morning I'll speak to the foreman.'

'Sandlal will laugh at you. Boy, you too stupid. Why you don't bathe and forget me?'

'Well, what you want here? Anybody does bathe in public?'

'This is public?' she said, erupting into laughter again. Then

105

she became serious and said, 'Listen, eh, I going.' She looked about her on the grass. The shadows were a little sharper now and above I could hear still more macaws and parakeets going home. I watched Sonia as she looked about her, and it came to me, could it be that she wanted me to be daring to her? These things happened. This case looked as clear as crystal. My thoughts were broken by Sonia saying, 'Oh!' and she stooped and picked up a cocoa-rod from the grass. She looked at me, relief on her face.

'So you really lost it?' I said surprised.

She mimicked: 'So you really lost it?' Then she said. 'What a little boy like you want with picking cocoa anyway.'

'What you mean?' I was right back to normal now.

'Well you should be going to school.'

'School on holidays,' I said, 'besides, I'd be sixteen in March and I'll leave school in any case.'

'Well, you in this cocoa-picking thing a long while now. You don't like school or what?'

'It's not that, but, you know, the money handy too bad.'

'Oh, Christmas money.'

'Aha.'

'And what you'll be doing after Christmas?'

'Pick more cocoa,' I laughed.

'Boy, you laughing – I don't know. You too young for this. I just don't know.'

'Look,' I said, leaving the water, 'my father don't want me to do this job either, but what else a man could do in Mayaro?'

'Well, if – '

I jumped back into the water and set Sonia rocking with laughter. My head was wild with shock and embarrassment. I had completely forgotten my nakedness, being carried away with talk, and I had walked right out of the stream.

'Don't be silly,' she said now, 'if you coming to put on your clothes, come and put on your clothes.'

I did not say anything but began rinsing myself. I pushed out in the water and made a few strokes. I dog-swam a little and I turned round and did the crawl. Then I stood up again, hoping she would go.

She said, laughingly: 'Just imagine you trying to hide from me. You know how many times I see that kinda thing? Nothing special about it. Anyway, I really have to go now.'

She moved off with the cocoa-rod. Somehow, I felt silly. 'See you tomorrow,' she called.

'Okay.' I was leaving the water.

I stood on the bank, dripping, watching Sonia disappear along the track. She did not even look back.

I had nothing to dry my skin with so I started jumping to shake the water off me. I made believe I was skipping and I spun the imaginary rope over my head and under my feet, and I crossed several times, backwards and forwards, with the imaginary rope.

Soon I was almost dry and I slung the imaginary rope into the bushes. My hair was still wet, though, and I rubbed it with my hands and it made my hands very wet. Somehow I was feeling very wholesome about Sonia now that she had gone. It was almost a shock to find her so natural and easy. She was not unsettled by my nakedness but took it as a joke. It did not matter to her. She had not come back for me to be daring to her as I had begun to think. She was the second person I had met who was so much like my father. I thought I would tell Joan about it when I wrote to her that night.

I had also written to ask Joan about coming here to visit. My mother had agreed to it very easily, and in fact she was rather amused. I had believed her to know a lot more than she really knew. Many times, on coming from work, she had met me talking with Rosalie Gidharee by the cashew tree, but she had made nothing of this, and on the day Pa had spoken to her about Joan she was most surprised to hear I had known about girls.

When I came in from work that evening she looked me over from head to foot and said, 'So you have girl-friend, then, Shell? Well, I never!' She couldn't stop laughing.

'He's a big man,' Pa said.

'Yes, yes – I have to agree with you there,' my mother said. She was teasing. She had been very cheerful, and I supposed it was the Christmas spirit that had put her in that mood. She said to my father, 'Hm! We'll soon have a wedding in this house.'

Pa did not give his 'hey-hey' laugh now, nor would he joke about this, and he said, 'The boy's only fifteen. Plenty time for marrieding.'

'So what! They does get married at fifteen these days, yes.'

'I don't want this boy to get marriage in his head now. What I want him to do is to get away from that dam' cocoa. What he want with marriage now? He could mind wife?'

'Take it easy,' my mother said, 'I was only joking with you.'

'I don't like to joke when it come to that.'

'All right, all right,' my mother said.

I could see in my father's eyes that he was thinking hard; and then he was a little more relaxed, and he said, 'But I mean he could bring his little girl-friend home and thing.'

'Oh yes. Of course. Let him bring them home.' She looked across at me, 'Bring all of them home,' she said.

My father laughed, 'Hey-hey!'

I was excited, seeing them in this mood, and I said, 'O God, Ma, you said *all* of them?'

'Yes, why not. Bring them.'

'Well, I mean somebody does only have *one* girl-friend.'

My mother looked across at my father and smiled and shook her head. My father said, 'Don't say nothing. Let him think that way. That's good. I like that.' And he laughed, 'hey-hey' again.

I said, 'Oh, I know a man don't *have* to have one girl, but, you know.'

My mother bent her head, laughing. She did not want me to see her laughing. My father said to her, 'Don't *say* nothing. I tell you don't tell him anything. Let him take that line.'

My mother had said absolutely nothing.

I had rarely seen them in such spirits. For my father it meant he was definitely feeling better. His belly did not look much heavier, and even though he was sitting up he did not look as one big with child. Which was a change. He was going to be okay over this Christmas. I was happy.

'Pa, you definitely staying till Saturday after New Year's?'

'Yes. Why?'

'No, I think it would be best to get Joan down some time around then.'

My mother said, 'Bring her down for New Year's.' She had her back to us and she was stooping and putting things into the cupboard. It was Monday in the week before Christmas but she had already done a little Christmas shopping. She had bought a little york ham – a four-pounder – and she took it up now in her hand and looked at it. Then she put it into the cupboard again. Then she looked around for me. 'Yes, man, New Year's. What you say – eh?'

I was secretly overjoyed. Pa had lain down a little and he seemed to be listening.

'I'll write tonight,' I said, 'she might come.'

Pa said, 'This Shellie ain't satisfied, you know. Bet he want to bring her down for Christmas.'

'No. No. I satisfied,' I said.

'He could bring her down anytime,' Ma said, 'but only that for Christmas everybody like to be home with their own family.'

'Ma it's all right. I'll bring her for New Year's – if she could come.'

'Bring her anytime,' Ma said.

She was finished packing away the things now and she stood up. She was big-boned and sturdy and yet she was truly feminine. When Pa had been badly ill and had to be taken to hospital she had become as thin as a rake. Now she was almost normal.

I looked at her stealthily. Her face had a very pleased look and she was looking at the walls of the room. She had a comb stuck in her hair. Most times when she was at home there was a comb stuck in her hair. When she sat combing her hair there was always something she could think of doing. So she got up and did it. Now she could find nothing to do with the walls. She had newly papered them herself – the first time in years we had been able to buy wall-paper for this. Formerly we used the picture pages of magazines. I looked at the walls and I too was well satisfied. I had stripped down the old magazine pages for her. She had stuck the paper on dead straight and where she had cut, the pattern corresponded exactly. The house looked like Christmas.

'You house looking like Christmas, Ma,' I said.

'Yes,' she said.

I felt she was also pleased because this Christmas I was able to put ten dollars in her hand. It was not only the money she valued but she valued also that I should give it to her. Though I could not see why not. I knew she felt this because she had told Rosalie's mother about it, and Rosalie told me. She and my father did not like me to work in the cocoa plantation, but there it was, I had given her ten dollars, and we had papered the walls, and we'd be able to buy drinks this Christmas, and I might even be able to ask my friends over, and there'd be a lot to eat. I liked a lot to eat at Christmas and this Christmas I would eat like a pig. My mother sat down now, combing her hair, as there was nothing at all to do. Outside, the dusk had come to Pierre Hill and I saw the flickering light of lamps through the curtains. My father was lying on the little bed with his eyes closed. Maybe he was asleep. I was thinking of Joan, and I would write to her when my mother went to bed. On Wednesday next there would be no work and I had already arranged to go to Cedar Grove with Mr Gidharee. I got up now and went on the step in the gloom and looked out. Around Pierre Hill the night was black but the sky was alive with stars. I thought of Rosalie Gidharee a little. All this vast place here before me, and the vastness behind me, and all the cocoa plantations and coconut plantations, and forest, around us, was Mayaro. I felt very tiny. The air was crisp and a little chilly because of the December wind. There was a streak of cheerfulness in me. I was thinking of Joan and of the Christmastime.

18

On Wednesday morning, by the time the mêlée of the dogs in the road reached our house, I was all set, and I walked out to meet Mr Gidharee in the road.

'Hello me old Shell,' he said, 'so you dress up for the old bush today, eh?'

I had on a thick blue-dock shirt and blue-dock trousers and I was wearing goloshes that I had bought to work in the cocoa-field with. They were the best thing for the prickles, and my feet felt nice and cool in them. He did not see that I also had a cutlass case, aud this was hanging from my belt on my left side. I turned on the side and said to him, 'How you like this?'

He was flabbergasted. 'Well what the hell is this?' he said. 'Shellie dressed to kill!' We laughed.

We carried on up the hill. The dogs knew me so well now that Rover was walking and rubbing against my legs. I stroked him a little and he pricked up his ears. I took his lead from Mr Gidharee and I let him walk against my leg, on the edge of the grass.

Mr Gidharee was still looking at me and admiring, and after a while he said, 'But you should be wearing longs, though. Why you don't go in for longs?'

'I order longs,' I said. 'A good pants. Serge. To go out in.'

'You should make all your pants longs,' he said. 'You tall enough for long pants now.'

'You think so?'

'Yes, you tall enough for longs. Look – ' He came alongside me to measure himself and he was only a little taller than I was. I was reaching up to his ears. 'Look, you tall as me already, boy, I don't see why you still wearing short pants for.'

A sudden bark from Tiger made me jump and the dog lunged forward, jerking its lead away from Mr Gidharee's hand. Then the three other dogs got excited and tried to follow and we had to pull hard to hold them back.

'Tiger!' Mr Gidharee called. Tiger had disappeared in the guava patch beside us.

We stood up, holding the other dogs short. Mr Gidharee was fuming. 'You see that blasted Tiger?' he said.

'It's that pig that run across the road.'

After a little while there was a continuous squealing and Mr Gidharee called 'Tiger!' at the top of his voice. The word had hardly died away before Tiger burst out of the guava patch again. The dog stood there, on the other side of the drain, looking up into Mr Gidharee's face.

'Come here,' Mr Gidharee said.

Tiger stood there wagging his tail but would come no further. He knew he had done something wrong and would not come.

'Come here,' Mr Gidharee said nicely, 'come here, Tiger, boy, I wouldn't break your backside.'

Tiger wagged his tail more violently and he jumped over the drain and into the road. Mr Gidharee took hold of the lead again.

'You is a hell of a dog. Hunting pig!' He laughed. 'I don't want you to hunt pig – pig *tame*. I want you to hunt wild meat. Like lappe and deer. Catch deer, for Christ sake, not *pig*.' And he roared with laughter.

He raised his hand to flick back his hair and Tiger jumped back. 'Stupid!' Mr Gidharee said, 'What you frighten for? If I say I wouldn't break you backside I wouldn't break you backside.'

Tiger then came on, and we went along again. Thinking over it, I could not help laughing to myself. Then I remembered the squealing we had heard in the bushes and I thought of the little pig, and I said, 'You think he kill it? The little pig.'

'Nah!' Mr Gidharee said, 'Tiger wouldn't kill it. You think Tiger stupid? He know the difference between pig and wild-beast. He was only sky-larking.'

We were close to Spring Flat now. Lion, Rover and Hitler were all walking on the grass, because of the hot pitch, but Tiger was on the pitch, with his nose to the ground and his ears pricked. He seemed to have completely forgotten the scolding he had got. He looked like a prize-dog, with his clean, spotted coat. None of these dogs had sores or fleas. They were in peak condition and powerfully strong. Especially Rover. Sometimes trying to check Rover was like trying to check a young bull.

113

As soon as we came to Cedar Grove I saw there was the redness of immortelle flower between the green of the trees. All over the macadam road, the fallen immortelle flowers made a layer of red, and in places, there were the yellow flowers of the poui. I knew that some kinds of immortelles bloomed at Christmas time, and others, towards the end of the dry season, but I was still surprised. The place looked picturesque.

We had freed the dogs and for the moment they had all disappeared into the bushes. Every now and again their barking came to us. As we walked along Mr Gidharee turned to me and said, 'You going to that fair New Year's Day, Shell?'

'I don't really know yet.'

'Rosalie was talking about it last night. Think she say she's going.'

'Oh yes?'

'Yes, man.' He nodded his head. I looked at him and his eyes were full upon me and I looked away. He said, 'Ro doesn't like to miss any school fête like that. She was talking about it just last night.'

'Oh,' I said.

'When I was young like you, boy, I never miss any school fête, you know,' he said, smiling.

I did not say anything. I was surprised to hear that Rosalie was going to that fair because that was the RC School's fair and not Government School's. Usually, the RC School pupils did not go to the Government School fairs and the Government School pupils never went to the RC's. The main reason for this was that the two schools were in different areas and the pupils of one hardly knew the pupils of the other. Also, there was a certain amount of school pride in it. It was odd that Rosalie should now say she was going to our fair because we had talked about this fair and she had not said she was going. I had written

114

to Joan about coming down for New Year's and I'd said I'd take her to that fair. I was not very happy now to hear that Rosalie was going to be there. Thinking about this I became uneasy. It was only after Mr Gidharee and I had walked down the track and had come to the red boundary flowers, with me being surprised by the wild greenness of the place before me. that the question of the fair slid from my mind.

Not having been to Mr Gidharee's little plantation for some time was enough to make the place look entirely strange to me. The potato slips we had planted were now huge vines which spread green and thick over their beds, and the cassavas had grown tall and stout in their rows. Also, Mr Gidharee had planted runner *bodi* peas and had made arbours for them and they had made one end of the plot a wilderness of curling, twisting vines. Near the cassava trees were quite a lot of tomato plants already in fruit, with the fruit huge, and green, and weighing down the limbs. The rice plots had now been cleared completely, and Mr Gidharee had not sown the new rice yet, and the earth here was forked up, and in parts, evenly moulded, and rich-brown. The whole place was greatly changed, and now, as I looked around, there was even sugar-cane – a few young shoots – which was not there before.

We were now walking along the little path which had been the edge of the rice-field, and I said, 'But you did a lot of work here since last time.'

'Last time is a long time,' he said.

There was not the strong smell of star-apples now, and looking up where they had been I could not see a fruit on the star-apple trees. Star-apples always seemed to burst into season suddenly and finish just as suddenly. There were a few oranges on the trees but these, too, were going out of season. The banana trees had young fruit. Now it was going to be the turn of the mangoes. The mango trees were flowering profusely, their tops smothered in yellow, and I did not mention this, but it was only now I had realised there was mango here.

We reached the shed and here was Tiger lying in front of the door. Not far away from him stood Hitler, the black, handsome dog. As Mr Gidharee opened the door, Lion appeared as if from nowhere, and squeezed past him and went inside. This made it three dogs with us, and I supposed Rover was in the bushes.

Mr Gidharee said, 'Sit down, boy. Let's sit down and rest a little.' There was a low plank placed across two horizontal pieces of wood and Mr Gidharee was sitting down on that. I sat too.

'Today we have to plant like hell, you know,' he said. There were several sacks in the shed and he looked at those now and I said, 'What you planting today – peas?'

'Everything. *Toute bagaille.* You know any patois?'

'A little bit. I know what *toute bagaille* is.'

He smiled, 'Well that's what we planting today, Shell boy. *Everything.* Just take a look in those bags.'

I got up and I looked into the sacks. Some had corn, some had dasheen slips, tania slips, and cassava stems; some had red beans, and black-eye peas, and pigeon peas, and there was a sack with some young banana shoots in it. There were a few other sacks which I did not open, for now he said to me, 'You smelling anything?'

'Yes.' From the time I had come into the shed there was the strong pleasant smell but I had not said anything.

'What you smelling.'

'Sapotee.'

'Well look at Shellie, eh!' he said, laughing. 'Your nose good, boy.'

'Where's the sapotee?' I said. I was sniffing the air.

'Well follow you nose, boy. Take up the scent.'

I sniffed again, then I bent and looked under the plank. As I bent down the smell of the ripening sapodillas was so strong it might have knocked me over. I pulled out the old hamsack from under the plank and I looked at Mr Gidharee and we grinned. I took out about five sapodillas and I put the hamsack back.

Mr Gidharee said, 'You just like me, boy – you like sapotee.'

'I like them too bad. Look – Rover come back.'

Rover had come into the shed now and he joined Lion. He lay down beside the brown dog and stretched out. Mr Gidharee just looked at him and said nothing. My sapodillas were as sweet as syrup.

Mr Gidharee got up and went over to the sacks of seeds and plant-slips, looking at the seeds especially, and as I sat there eating sapodillas, I was listening to the birds outside. There were not so many of them now as when the fruit was in full swing, and now, above us, there was not wild screeching, but the clear and distinct whistling of the songster birds. I was listening particularly to a semp. It was singing rather than twittering. Every note came clear and pure, and as I sat listening, my thoughts went back to those times when I used to catch birds, and I began remembering how I used to make my cages from *bois-canoe* stalks, and how I used to bleed *lagley* gum from breadfruit trees, and set the stickiest *lagley* all round the top of my cage, and perch my cage, with my best semp inside, right on the top of a pole, in the bushes, and how I would hide myself away, listening to my semp calling the other birds. As soon as a bird was lured to rest on the cage, and got itself stuck on the *lagley* I would pounce out from my hiding place.

For singing, semps and tarodes I liked better than any others. The *jeune male* was all right, but when it began to turn *vieux male* that was the time it became pretty. I wondered how much Mr Gidharee knew about birds. If I met someone who knew about birds I could talk on the subject for six months. I looked

117

across at Mr Gidharee and he was deeply absorbed in his plant-slips and seeds, his lips moving, and for a moment I thought I would hold a conversation about birds with him – and then I thought not. Lion amused me a little, the way he lay so comically on the ground. Like a child. Rover had got up and gone, I did not know when. Thinking about cage-birds I had almost forgotten these dogs. I looked at Lion, the way he sprawled himself out. Every now and again he pawed his belly to chase away some fly. His coat was a nice brown – a sort of reddish brown – rather like a deer's. My father had a jacket almost the same colour. Of all the dogs of Mr Gidharee, Lion was the gentlest. Tiger was the mad one.

The birds were still singing in the trees – especially that semp. Also, now from far away came the tock-tock of a wood-pecker. They called them 'carpenter birds', and no name could be more apt. It was odd, though, I had only rarely seen wood-peckers.

'If you want more sapotee you could take, you know,' Mr Gidharee said.

His voice made me jump. 'No, it's all right.'

'You rest enough? You ready for a little sweating now?'

'Yes – if you like.' I got up.

'You well gingery this morning.'

'Yes, I just feel like it.'

'Oh, you feel like it? I'll work you like a bitch today, boy – come on!'

I laughed.

We took up the hoe and the sacks and other things and I followed Mr Gidharee outside. The sun was very hot and where it came through the leaves of the trees onto the ground, the place seemed splintered with silver. Tiger was out here and lying on his back in a patch of sun, and Hitler, with his nose to the ground, was walking along the edge of the river as though he was on patrol.

We went to the part near the river which was prepared for the pigeon peas. Mr Gidharee showed me how he wanted them planted – three to a hole. Although we had not begun working yet his face was already greasy with sweat. When he bent down now his hair fell over in front of his eyes, and he jerked his head back sharply to throw the hair in place again. Then he got down to the job and his hands moved like lightning.

After working a little while I stood up to straighten my back, and I turned round and looked at the river. Dark, dreamy Ortoire eased along. There were pieces of wood upon it, and bits of green branches, and sometimes a log, and very often something black sticking out of the water – which – God help us! – could be an alligator's snout. I did not think of this much now, for I was remembering something I had seen in Freddie's café just the other night. A picture. It was of night falling upon a sea and there was no ship but lots of things floating on the water. Looking at the river now made me think of this. I bent down again to the planting, and I said quietly, 'The Flotsam and Jetsam of the Sea'

'What?'

'Nothing. Just something I was thinking about.'

'It's only crazy people who does talk to themselves.'

'No, it's just a picture in Freddie's café. You know that picture – the sea picture on the wall over the ice-box?'

'Aha.'

'I was just remembering it.'

He looked at me, puzzled. He stood up to straighten his back. 'Why?'

'Don't really know.'

He chuckled. 'Boy if you ain't crazy you ain't far.'

That made me chuckle.

The sun was beating down now, and I myself was beginning to perspire. This part near the river was not very much shaded, and the sun had climbed right overhead. I was listening to the birds in the trees and for some odd reason I was again thinking of the song-birds I used to catch. I was wondering why was it we gave our Trinidad birds French names. Like *jeune male* and *vieux male*. The *vieux male* was very beautiful with yellow under its belly and blue on its back and wings. It was very beautiful but it had already lost its singing voice. But when it was young it sung fine. That's to attract the female, I thought. The girls. But even then it could not touch the semp, for notes. I did not think I would keep birds any more, though. I was too old for that.

I looked towards Mr Gidharee. He was a little way down past me, having done that much more work than me. 'What is *jeune male*? I mean in English.'

He looked at me, grinning. His face was shining with sweat. 'You is a patois man and you don't know that?'

'I don't know a lot of patois. We don't talk so much patois down-the-beach.' In fact, I was just testing his patois knowledge.

'But still, *jeune male*, that so simple. Well listen, what is a *jeune male* – the young little bird, or the old one?'

'The young one.'

'Well that's it. *Jeune male* – young male.'

'Oh, I see.'

He turned round to his planting again, looking very satisfied.

One of the strange things was that you hardly found Indian people speaking French patois. Mr Gidharee was what they called 'perfectly creolised'. He' was not merely pretending he knew patois. I could sense that he knew it well, from the way he pronounced *jeune male*. Having already said I knew only a little patois, I could not now strike up a conversation in it. I turned to my work and said nothing for a while.

Just past noon we finished planting the peas on the little

section of plot. Mr Gidharee had worked it out so precisely that the space was just enough for the amount of peas we had. As we got up to go to the shed by habit I looked round for the dogs. None of them were around and presently a little yapping came from the bushes. Mr Gidharee said, Wait a minute, and he went and brought the calabash from the shed then he went down to the riverside and dipped it full. He poured water for me to wash my hand, then I poured for him. Then he filled the calabash again so he could give the dogs to drink. As we came back from the riverbank he whistled, 'Phee-O Phee-O!' and at once I could hear the tumbling in the bushes, and the yapping and the next moment the first of the dogs leaped into the yard of the shed. He poured water into their bowl and he said, 'Now no fighting – every man take his time!' Rover and Lion were lapping up the water.

'Shell, what about that school-fête, you taking Rosalie?' Mr Gidharee said, without looking round.

I was so surprised by the question, I just said, 'Yes.'

19

Christmas morning came very softly to Pierre Hill. When I woke up and went outside there were hardly any sounds at all. The sun was bright on the pitch, and in the yard the shadow of the lime tree was pierced with slices of light. The mango tree had already dropped all its bloom and now there were bunches of young mangoes camouflaged among the leaves. Right across the low-lying land to the other side on the hill I could see the coconut trees rustling, and there was the dazzle of glass windows from the big red-topped house. The houses around were bright with new curtains.

I went and sat on the grass in the shade of the lime tree. I could hear my mother stirring inside. Occasionally, from the other side of the hedge there came noises from over at the neighbour's. She seemed to be chopping wood. Usually she lived alone, but last night relations had come. There was a great deal of talking and laughing over there last night.

Out in the road, now, the sun was bright, almost dazzling, off the pitch. It was such a warm, quiet Christmas morning, I just wanted to lie down and sleep on the grass. I lay back, with my eyes open, and there was the great dome of blue above my head. I was thinking of last night. We had had a lovely time in Freddie's café. Joe had come home from Princes Town and Lennard was there also and we had what you called a good old talk, and Freddie bought wine and Lennard had fetched a flask of Vat 19 rum and we had drinks and Freddie gave us cigarettes. There was a group of carol-singers going round singing to the big-wigs. They went and sang at the Post Mistress's place, then they went up to the Doctor's residence, and then to old Bullin's, and they even went to the Police Station. When they passed in front of Freddie's café we called them 'crawlers' and all sorts of names.

After we had had a few drinks and had begun to feel merry we decided to walk all the way to the Catholic Church to hear the Midnight Mass. To see girls, really. The Catholic Church was at the place called 'Down-the-beach' – my own area – and I knew I would see girls I had not seen for months. Anyway, there was only one girl I was thinking about all the time and that was Joan. As we walked I told them about Joan, and Lennard was very amazed that things had developed so strongly. They all remembered how I was dancing with her on Discovery Day. Lennard could not get over the fact that Joan was now my girl, and he was delighted, and he asked me many questions about her – one for which I nearly punched him down. Everything was so delightful, walking with my friends in the dark, going down to the church. Smoking all the way. Feeling merry. Walking past brightly lit houses, with the smell of baking cakes, and liquor, and boiling hams, in the air. Walking through coconut groves with fire-flies about. Everything felt so wonderful, being with Lennard and Joe and Freddie. Joe was the same old Joe, as if he had not gone to Princes Town at all ...

'Shellie.'

My mother's voice made me start. I turned on my belly. 'Yes?'

'You ain't hungry this morning or what?'

'Yes,' I lied.

'Look, I put everything out for you already. Come on, then.'

'One minute.'

'Come on if you coming.'

'Okay. Just a little minute.'

I wanted to lie down a little bit more on the grass and go through last night again. Funny how the thoughts had taken possession of me and had begun to sweeten me so much. Yesterday was really a nice Christmas Eve. A bright, busy Christmas Eve. Down at the junction by the shops there were people like ants. Thick and swarming like ants. You'd have never thought there were so many people in Mayaro. And afterwards, when darkness began to fall, you heard the little boys 'bursting' carbide. The boom-boom of the carbide exploding in old ovaltine tins came from every direction, and sometimes you saw the glow of the explosion. I was too old even for this, now, but it made me remember childhood days.

'Shellie, you ain't coming or what!'

'Coming, Ma.'

'Stop that coming and come.'

I got up from the grass at last and brushed my behind.

My mother said, 'Look, if you still want to sleep go to your bed, eh? After all that ruction you made last night you can't keep up now!'

'What ruction? I only came in a bit late.' I squeezed past her, into the house.

'A bit late? You didn't come in late at all. You came in very early. Very early in the morning!'

I laughed. She was right, too. I hoped she would not carry on with this talk. Everything on the table looked like Christmas. Ma had baked last night and on the table was nice home-made bread and ham and chocolate tea. There was also a cloth with fine-ground ginger heaped upon it and on the window-sill there was the huge decanter of ginger-beer in the sun. The ginger-beer was supposed to be still setting and there was a white cloth over the top of the decanter. There was a shelf above the window and on this Ma had laid out all the chinaware and a few wine glasses. I looked at all these things now to avoid my mother's eyes because I knew she was not finished with me.

After much staring about, my eyes found hers again. She was looking at me and she had a faint, disbelieving smile on her face.

'What's it now, Ma?'

She just shook her head. Then she said, 'So you does go out now and drink and get drunk? Since you working in the cocoa you is a big man?'

'I wasn't really drunk last night, you know.'

'Who wasn't drunk? You asking me or telling me!'

'I only had about two or three little drinks.'

'Who you was with?'

'Freddie and the boys.'

'I mean all night.'

'Yes. You could ask Freddie.'

'Well *he* brought you home, so I – '

'He brought me home?'

She looked dumbfounded: 'So who brought you home last night, mister?'

This startled me. I tried to think but in my mind that part of last night was a blank. All I could remember was up to the time we were walking back from the church. I would have sworn that I had come home normally.

'I don't know,' I said. I was not laughing now.

She laughed. 'Anyway, it's Christmas. And you is not a "goodtime" boy – I can't say that. Eat up – and then you'll give me a hand in the kitchen.'

'What happen to Pa – he ain't get up yet?'

'Get up? Go and have a look. He sleeping as if he dead there.'

'It's that soft bed. I'll wake him up.'

'No, leave him.'

'Good Christ, it's big Christmas Day.'

'So what. You let him sleep a little more. He have the whole day before him. And you drop that "Christ", please.'

I thought of Pa still lying there, sleeping. This was most unusual for him. Although he hadn't worked for years he was always up with the break of day. I wondered if it was the softness of our big bed.

I went to the table and things were nice but I did not eat much of the breakfast. I went into the bedroom now to have a look at Pa.

He lay sprawled there in a deep sleep. It was rather odd for this was the first time in my memory Pa had slept on this bed. Because of his illness, the small bed which we called the settee was much more convenient, and he always slept there, in the sitting room, even from Down-the-Beach days. The fact that he was here on the bed showed how well he was feeling and that he could climb up on the bed. Now in his pyjamas he looked like a young boy. He had had his hair trimmed and Ma had shaven him, herself, and last night must have been the first time in years that he had cuddled my mother. He was shorter than I was now, you could tell that. I had grown quite a lot lately. Looking at him now you could never guess he had a son of fifteen. Somehow today he did not look at all ill and his belly was not bulging. Anyway, at the moment he was knocked out with sleep.

'Shell,' my mother called from the kitchen.

'Yes.'

'I said not to wake him up, you know.'

'All right.'

'Come on, then.'

'All right.'

The bedroom was spotless and tidy – everything fixed away nicely and new sheets on the bed. The floor was scrubbed. I went out again into the sitting room then down the side steps into the kitchen. Here was a strong scent of cloves and chive and other food seasoning and this put me in a sudden light-hearted mood. Ma said, 'Come and hold this here for me.' It was the cock she had killed and she wanted me to hold it in a certain way so she could chop it up properly.

'Ma, O Christ, let's have a drink first, nuh – I mean, it's *Christmas Day.*'

'Well look at this boy!' she said, putting down the knife and taking the kitchen cloth to wipe her hand. 'Okay, go and get it. Bring a madeira and two glasses. Or if *you* want rum. Don't take the new glasses, you know.'

I brought the wine and the glasses into the kitchen and I handed her a glass. I knocked the bottom of the bottle against my heel to push the cork. Ma was looking at me closely. I was smiling. I drew up the rest of the cork with my teeth and I began to pour into her glass. 'Say when,' I said. It was not a large glass and when it was nearly full she said, 'When.' I filled up my own glass. She looked at it and said, 'Careful, you know – you know you ain't have no head for drink.'

'That's what Freddie said.'

'Oh, Freddie said that? Well, take heed.'

'Don't mind Freddie. Cheers, Ma. Cheerio.' I tried to knock my glass on hers.

'Well look at this boy!' she said. 'You think I is any drunkard with you!'

She put her glass for me to knock it and I said, 'Good health.'

'Good health. Merry Christmas.'

'Merry Christmas. Good health to Pa.'

This last made her go suddenly delicate and I said no more. We drank up and she started cutting up the fowl. She forgot she had wanted me to hold it for her. I took the bottle inside again and as I went in I could hear Pa stirring in the bedroom.

I called to Ma, 'Pa up,' and I went into the bedroom.

He was sitting on the edge of the bed and his eyes seemed screwed-up with sleep. 'Merry Christmas, Pa.'

'Merry Christmas, boy. O God, I sleep like the devil.'

'That's good. That's all right. What's wrong with that?'

'What's the time like?'

'About nine so.'

'Where you mother?'

'In the kitchen.'

He slid down from the bed.

'You all right, Pa? I mean, you want me to help you change?'

'Oh no. I all right.'

'You want to take a little drink with me?' I said, and at once I could have bitten my tongue, for here was my mother coming into the bedroom.

'Your father just get up and you talking about drink?'

'All right. All right.'

I went out of the bedroom.

'Shell!' my father called. I went back. He said, 'First things first. Bring that bottle.'

'Don't bring no bottle here,' my mother said. 'We'll have a hell of a row here this Christmas morning. You just wake up and you talking about drinking rum!'

When Ma talked like that she meant it. I cleared out and went into the yard and this time I sat down in the sun.

I was feeling very good, somehow. The sun was bright and although the day was more alive now, it was still serene. Over the hedge, at our neighbour's, there seemed to be much bustle, and already the odour of cooking was floating across to our place. Then from further down the road a gramophone started up. At first I could not tell where the music was coming from, but from the time I recognised the record, I knew. It was coming from the Gidharees'. From the time you heard the calypso, *Hold your hand, Madame Khan*, it was the Gidharees playing it. They played it so often I almost knew the words by heart. Since we had moved here I must have heard that record a thousand times.

The sun was beginning to burn the skin so I dragged on my bottom until I came to the shade of the lime tree. There was a calabash tree across the road. Underneath it, the place was white with the flowers of Christmas bush.

It was a nice feeling to look at this and think about Christmas, and I was thinking aimlessly when all of a sudden I remembered the plan I had made with Freddie and the boys in the café last night. We were all going to each other's home today. First, they were coming to mine, after lunch. Then we'd go to Lennard's, then to Joe's and Freddie's last. I got up and went round the house to the kitchen to Ma.

As soon as she saw me she said, 'Where you was all the time?'

'Just outside, under the lime tree.'

'You father calling you for a drink.'

128

'Oh, I didn't hear.' Before going in to him I said, 'By the way, the fellers coming up here after lunch – Joe and Lennard and Freddie. Okay?'

'A fine time to tell me!'

'I forgot clean, O jeese!'

'It's all right. I only joking,' she said.

I had a drink with my father, and then I went back out into the yard. And then feeling completely idle, I went out into the road. There was absolutely nothing happening on this road this Christmas morning. Looking to the left, as the road swept up the hill, and to where it dipped out of sight on its way to Cedar Grove, there were about four or five stray dogs lying on the pitch. To the right, towards the junction where the shops and cafés were, there were only one or two people about. The place looked very deserted.

As I stood there my eyes wandered to the cashew tree, and seeming to see little pink things on the limbs, I walked down to it. Yes, the cashew tree was getting into blossom again. And the green thing like moss on the branches was young leaves. I was thrilled by this. Underneath the tree where the ground had been trampled bare only a few months ago, there was much grass and weeds.

I sat down on the bank over the drain and I was looking up into the tree. Presently I heard a bark and I looked across the road. It was Lion and Rosalie at the Gidharees' gate. Lion was not on a lead but she was holding him by the collar and he was frisking about with her.

She brought him across the road and I could see she was coming towards me. There was something like a parcel under her left arm. She was wearing a blue skirt and white sailor bodice and she looked rather charming this morning.

'Merry Christmas,' I said, when she was quite near.

'Merry Christmas.'

When she got under the tree she let go of Lion. 'What you doing out here?' she said.

'Nothing, really. Just had a little drink and I felt like cruising out for a little fresh air, you know.'

'What you was drinking?'

'Oh, I had a madeira with Ma, and me and Pa had a Vat 19.'

'You like wine?' she asked, rather anxiously.

She was looking very cheerful and pretty.

'Yes. Why?'

She took out the parcel from under her arm. 'I was wondering if you does drink wine. I buy this "Fruity Muscatel". For your Christmas.'

She offered me the bottle in the paper-bag. I was very surprised. 'O God, Rose, you shouldn't do that.' I refrained from taking it.

'Oh come on. I buy it just for you so you *have* to take it.'

'Oh *Rosalie*!' I said. I had great misgivings, but I stretched out my hand and took it. As I held the bottle her hand touched mine and my heart jumped. Her finger stayed on mine and she was looking at me with her dark expressive eyes. I rested the bottle down beside me, my heart thumping.

I said. 'Look, Rosalie, I hope you don't mind, but this year I ain't buy any Christmas presents for nobody, you know, so I feel funny to take this.'

'That ain't nothing.'

I took up the bag and I took the bottle from it and looked at the muscatel. It had one of those sealed corks that you could never draw without the cork breaking. Most times, in the end, you had to push it down. On the label of the bottle there was the picture of three keys and over them it said, 'Old Fruity Muscatel'. I felt very touched that Rosalie should give me this present, and in a way I was very embarrassed.

130

'You know Joe here?' I said.

'Yes, yes.' And then she said, 'He sent me a card quite from Princes Town.'

'Oh yes? You know I didn't even send anybody any Christmas card this year. And yesterday I got one.'

'From who?'

I had not foreseen this question but it struck me in a flash that now was the time to let her know.

'From a girl named Joan.'

Rosalie's face changed. 'Who's that? Anybody I know?'

'You remember that Discovery Day fair?'

'Aha.'

'Well she was there. I think we even showed her to you. It's a girl from Sangre Grande.'

'I see.'

Having got this far I felt very relieved. Rosalie was just staring at me. She had never actually said she liked me but now she was looking at me so icily it was as though I had done a crime. Then she was staring at the grass. Then she said, 'You two in something?'

'Yes.'

'Oh,' she said. She pursed her lips and looked very thoughtful.

I said, 'So you sent Joe a card back?'

'Yes.'

'He used to write you from Princes Town?'

'I never answer those letters.'

'But why?'

'Just so.'

'But you used to be so crazy about him.'

'That was once upon a time.'

Lion was lying quietly on the grass. Now and again he shook his head violently or flapped his ears, to chase away the flies. I was trying to concentrate on him a little. I was growing quite infatuated with Rosalie as she stood here and I wanted to stem this. I did not have much experience in being close to girls who liked me – and who I was inclined to like. Maybe this meant something. As I looked at her I realised that she, too, had developed quite fast. She was much more a young woman now than when I had first come to Pierre Hill. She had straps at her back as well. She had taken on all the actions of a woman, and she had something like allure, something like temptation, and yet there was a quiet innocent charm. I tried to describe her in silence and it was very strange.

She said, 'The cashew tree getting flowers again, you notice?'

'Oh, yes girl.' I came right back to the moment.

She bent back looking at the cashew tree and as I looked at her there were the two points pressing out the pockets of her sailor bodice, and it set me thinking how in one season we could be children, and in the next we could be grown. As I thought about her I began feeling alarmed about myself, for Joan was still everything to me.

'That's funny about your friend Joe,' I said. 'You is such a sweet jane and yet – and yet he so dam' slack.'

'Joe is a nice boy,' she said.

'And what happen then? I mean, what really happen?'

'You.'

'What?'

'Nothing.' She was suddenly shy about what she had said and now she could not look me in the face.

'I didn't get that, Ro.'

'You ask what happen. Well, nothing happen. So what? After one time is two, eh? People don't stay the same way all the time.'

'Anyway, that's you and Joe. It just look odd, that's all. He coming up by me after lunch. He and Lennard and Freddie. You coming over by us?

132

'Me? Why? Not me. If you want, *you* could come by us. But by yourself. You and Pa supposed to be friends.'

I did not want to go there, but I could not tell Rosalie so. I just did not want Mr Gidharee to get it too seriously in his head that I was after Rosalie.

I said. 'Well okay, you come by me and later on I'll come by you.'

'Look, Shell, I'll tell you this as a friend. You know about me and Joe and all that. But Joe was really a joker. And I don't really want to meet him face to face. I didn't really send him back any card and I didn't answer his letters and in any case this so-called boy-friend and girl-friend business was a lot of stupidness.'

'You mean the little soft-spot?'

'If you call it that.'

'He write to tell you anything out of the way?'

'Not really. You know Joe.'

I chuckled. I was thinking that that was exactly what Joe did wrong. He did not tell her anything out of the way. I was thinking to myself how delicious she looked today and I was wondering if Joe was blind or something. I said, 'Well listen, this evening, after the Christmas quiet down and thing, I'll see you up here, eh?'

'You coming over?'

'No, I'll meet you here – by this cashew tree, okay?'

'Okay,' she said.

'I think I'd better go home now. Perhaps the old lady wondering where I gone.'

'What about your Pa?'

'Oh, he's first-class today, girl.'

'Nice.' She bent down and held Lion by the collar and pulled him up. We had been there so long Lion had dropped asleep. Rosalie seemed to have a great deal of sparkle in her again.

133

'I said, 'Okay, then, so we'll see later?'
'Yes.'
'I mean, you'll be here, *definite*?'
'I'll be here.'
'I mean, come, you know. Don't make me come here and wait for nothing.'
'If I ain't coming I'll say I ain't coming,' she said.
'Okay, cheerio for now. I must go.'
'Bye.'

◆

I had a fine time with the boys. After Joe and Lennard and Freddie called on me after lunch and we had drinks, and after they wished my mother long life and my father good health, we left to go down to Lennard's place, and Joe's and Freddie's. Since Freddie's place was the nearest, we made the next visit there, and the truth was, once there, we had no chance of visiting Lennard's or Joe's. Freddie lived at the back of his café and he had two big rooms and a bedroom and a kitchen. We started drinking ginger-beer and then he brought out a crystal rum called 'Captain's Choice', and a bottle of carypton, and a bottle of sorrel wine which he had made himself. 'Captain's Choice' was a docile-looking rum, and very like water, in the bottle, but Freddie warned me it kicked like a mule.

Having already had a few drinks my tongue loosened easily and I began admiring Freddie's sitting rooms and the bedroom and I began talking of Joan and somehow Freddie got the idea that I wanted to bring Joan here. Lennard was highly delighted with this and he laughed obscenely, and Joe, who had lost all his shyness in Princes Town, began stirring up this talk and began asking me when, when. Freddie said I was one boy he'd arrange anything for and he said all this would cost me was a cinema ticket, because if he vacated his room he would have to occupy his time somehow. There was no cinema at Mayaro, but at Rio Claro there was this film, *Salome, Where She Danced*. Yvonne de Carlo. I told Freddie to go to hell.

As Freddie was talking to me he poured a little wine in my 'Captain's Choice'. Now this Freddie was a boy who said he liked me! I was not all that tipsy and I saw what he was doing. And I knew what I was about, too. I took up the glass and went to the window and poured out the rum-wine. Then I filled the glass with ginger-beer and tried to put it to my mouth. Lennard and Freddie were writhing with laughter. Joe was just looking at me closely. Now this Joe was truly my friend. He had been gay all along, but as soon as he saw me begin to look shaky he changed. Now he was sitting back, very calm and cool, and looking at me.

'Joe, you cool-brains?' I said.

'Always.'

Freddie said, '*You*, Shell?'

I looked at him, 'Having a royal time. Like the queen said.'

Lennard saw this as being funny and burst out laughing, and Joe smiled.

I said, 'Freddie, a man is a man, but if you think I'm bringing Joan here, you making the biggest mistake.'

'No, I mean it's up to you,' he said. He was using his hands a great deal now in talking. Not that he was drunk, but he was what we called 'high'. His hands looked like four hands to me. He said, 'I mean as friends I make a proposition.'

'Not that girl, boy.'

Joe turned to Lennard, 'She so nice as all that?' Joe had seen the girl at Discovery, but with Joe she might well have been a boy – for all he cared.

Lennard said, 'Of course she's nice. Who you think introduce him. That's the nicest jane in Sangre Grande, boy.'

Joe seemed to think of something, then he laughed, and then he said, 'If she so nice, Len, why you didn't keep her for yourself?' I watched those two and said nothing. Joe poured some wine into his glass now. As he tilted the bottle my mind went straight back to my Fruity Muscatel but I'd be damned if I'd speak of it now, with Joe sitting there. Even though I was tipsy.

'For one thing,' Lennard started to explain, 'any girl I get to be too friendie-friendie with, I can't tell her nothing out of the way. You know that? Freddie, you is a man who have experience – any girl who you start to talk to nice and innocent and thing, you just *can't* change the tune – right, Fred?'

Freddie nodded.

'This is a funny thing,' Lennard went on. 'And something else. Somehow, this Joan – I know she's nice and cute and all that, but somehow she doesn't – how you call it – she doesn't *shatter* me, you know what I mean. *Attract.*'

'She's a dam' nice first-class girl,' I said hotly

'Yes, I know.'

'So what the france you talking about?'

'She doesn't knock me down, that's all.'

'Because you don't blinking well – '

'Listen, Shell,' Freddie interrupted, 'listen to the man. He said the girl don't attract him. He don't mean she ain't nice. I mean all of us see the little thing in the dance Discovery Day and be-Christ she's a dam' nice jane. I for one give her full marks. But I know what Len mean. From the time you make yourself too friendly and *social*, like, with a girl – on the innocent side and thing – good God that's the worst thing.'

He was talking with the air of a philosopher. He was gesturing even more now than before, and I knew he was very 'high'. I happened to stop myself from becoming more tipsy by drinking straight fruit juice. And ginger-beer. Strictly non-alcoholics. All the time Freddie was talking Lennard was nodding his head in agreement. Joe had drunk out almost all the madeira single-handedly. He did not show the slightest sign of being drunk. They were all quiet for the moment, and I said, 'Anyway, Joe girl is a nice jane too.'

'You mean little Gidharee?' Freddie said.

'Aha.'

Freddie put up his thumb to show she was first-rate.

'Anyway she's not Joe girl,' I added. I did not know what made me say this. Somehow my tongue had been very impatient to say this. I wondered if I had hurt Joe's feelings, for he was looking outside now. Neither Freddie nor Lennard said anything. Somehow I knew my head had become lighter with the drinking and my tongue was urging me still further to say I was meeting her up by the cashew tree tonight. I kept biting my tongue for me not to say it because I was feeling very much to say it. I did not say it because I liked Joe so much.

'Joe, me boy, pass that madeira bottle there, boy,' I said.

Reaching for it from him I said,' Joe too dam' respectable, that's what. What you having Fred?'

'I'll have Vat.'

'Vat is Freddie middle name,' I explained. 'It's Vat or nothing for Freddie.'

The Vat 19 was in front of Lennard and he took up the bottle and held it up looking at it against the light, then he poured a fair measure into his own glass, and completely ignoring Freddie he rested the glass and the bottle down in front of him again.

'Pass the so-and-so bottle,' Freddie said.

'Language!' Joe said.

We all laughed.

We consumed a great deal of the liquor – not so much on my part – then Freddie suggested that we go out to the front. Because while we were sitting here we were missing a lot of the *scenery* passing by in the road – according to Freddie. That meant, girls. We cleared out for the front.

Here, at the front of the café, it was lively, and the December breeze was cool and the sun was shining palely on the road. It was about five o'clock now. There were quite a number of people about and they were all dressed up and almost everybody who passed by wished us a happy Christmas. I asked Freddie why he did not open his café today, since there so many strollers about, and he said he was going to open at six. He said he would not open before six on principle. I did not know on which principle, but that was what he said. I then asked Freddie how old he was for I had long been trying to puzzle out how was it we could be so chummy and easy with him and he with us and we were only very young fellows and Freddie was already a man. He said he was twenty-four. He looked very regretful.

While talking to me there was a group of girls coming from across the savannah and Freddie's face brightened.

'Look,' he said, 'Theresa and them. Let's invite them to a party. A *pelau*.'

'What *pelau*? Who will cook this *pelau*?' Lennard said.

'We.'

First we laughed, then we thought of it as being just possible, and then we were all keen for it. Joe said he was keen because he wanted to make as much ruction as he could before going back to Princes Town. Joe was supposed to be the shy one! Anyway, when the girls reached near, Freddie called them over. They were all Freddie's friends, and there was this one called Theresa and she was keen on the *pelau* idea. They were going for a walk down the beach but they would come back. Only they must go down to the beach to see what it looked like today. But they'd come back, sure, sure – okay? – Okay, matter fix, Freddie said. – Case? Case in bag, Freddie said. – Okay, case, then, Theresa said. They left us.

138

Having dreamed up the *pelau* all of a sudden and now having to live up to it, Freddie became very excited. He asked if we had any money to pool, and we did not have much. That meant we had to go home and come back with something. A bottle or two, he said. He would take care of the eats. He asked if any of us knew how to steal fowls. I took it for granted that he was joking but Lennard put up his hand. *He* wasn't joking. He took Freddie to the back and they talked. Joe and I laughed together. When Freddie came back he said, 'You know what? This bleddy café ain't opening tonight. On principle.' We laughed. He saw that Joe and I were getting excited about the *pelau* and he said, 'Let me tell you buggers in advance, this ain't going to be no bacchanal party, you know. Don't think this will be any brothel kinda thing. I have my name to keep up in this district. I is a decent man.'

'Okay, decent man,' Lennard said, and we roared with laughter. Joe was growing quite nervous about the party.

20

We had the *pelau* party and there was a lot of fun and singing, and it was far into the night before the party broke up. The girls had returned from their walk just before night-fall and we had heard the steel-bands coming out to serenade but we did not go out to watch. Freddie had got a few more of the boys to come to the party, and with everybody bringing along something we had more to eat and drink than we could manage. Theresa had taken charge of the cook-up. The girls were very merry but there was not what Joe had been expecting. At least not as far as I knew.

For I did not know how the party ended. When I awoke on Boxing morning I realised what had happened and could hardly face my parents. My father was very amused, but my mother was fuming cross.

'You know you ain't have no head for rum,' she said. 'When you go out for *God* sake don't drink!'

I remained quiet.

My father said, 'Let the boy strive. This is Christmas.'

'Yes, but he can't drink at all at all, and when this sort of thing happen, well you don't know what could happen to him. I mean I really getting frighten for him.'

Neither I nor my father spoke, and my mother said, 'With this boy, what's-his-name – Freddie – with Freddie I don't mind so much, because he seem all right, but you never know who you'll be drinking with.'

'You talking as if this boy is a drinker. He only having a good time because it's Christmas, that's all.'

'Well I only hope so,' my mother said.

All this while she was talking she was out in the kitchen. It was broad daylight and I had just opened my eyes and I found I had been sleeping on the little bed. My father had again slept in the bedroom and now he was already up and changed and out in the sitting room. I wanted to ask him who had brought me home but I did not. I was feeling awful. I had a bad headache and it was as if there was a typhoon inside my guts. Since my mother had mentioned Freddie I guessed it was Freddie who had brought me home last night. I had been so determined not to get drunk and that was what had happened! I half lay, half sat up on the little bed and I was feeling deep remorse.

'Want a little coffee?' my father said. I looked up at him. I saw he was watching me closely.

'Yes, Pa, please.'

He told my mother. She was in the kitchen, and I could tell, from the smell of frying ham, that she was getting my breakfast ready. I had a fitful sleep and my eyes were feeling tight. I sat up from my half-lying position and I felt a little dizzy and I held my head.

'You better take some Andrews,' my father said.

'No, I'm all right.'

'You take it.'

'All right.'

He took a glass from the cupboard and put some Andrews into it and he poured some water from the goblet into the glass. The sudden brightness on my eyes made me wince a little, but after a moment I was all right. There was a stray dog lying on the side of the road, just opposite me, with its mouth wide open, panting from the heat. While looking at the dog, I saw Mr Prefat coming along. Mr Prefat was one of the oldest men on Pierre Hill, and he was so old that he was bent, and he was hobbling rather than walking.

'Morning, Mr Prefat.'

'Morning.'

'You had a nice Christmas?'

'Not too bad, nuh. Not too bad, son, thank you.'

I watched him go by with his stick and his little hop-and-drop walk. I looked out on the green trees and the low-lying land between us and the high ground beyond. There was a cocoa-house in the distance and it was already open, with the beans exposed for drying. Normally, there would be people 'dancing' the cocoa to prevent the beans drying in clumps. No one was 'dancing' the cocoa today.

'Come on if you hungry,' my mother said.

She had brought my breakfast in and I went to the table. My father, for the want of doing something, was shining his shoes. But now he stopped to look at me again.

'Still feeling bad?'

'Yes.'

'Well eat and go back and lie down.'

I just was not feeling hungry any more. Maybe the trouble was I had not slept enough. I was feeling very vomity without the vomit even coming near. It was a long time since last I had felt this way. I drank up the coffee and left everything else and went and lay down.

I slept right through until the late afternoon of this Boxing Day. My father was in the house when I woke up, but my mother was out. Of course, my father could not possibly go anywhere. My mother who had not left the front door since Christmas Eve had gone down the beach to Radix to see an old friend. As I looked out of the front door I could see that the day was just about finished. There was darkness between the leaves of the trees, and now only the houses on the top of the hill, far on the other side, was in light. On Pierre Hill a few lamps were already lit. I could see them flickering through the windows of the houses. I was trying to listen to see if any music was coming from the Government School, for there was a Boxing Day annual Christmas Tree, Dinner, and Dance, for old folk, being held there. Sometimes if the wind was right you could hear if there was music in the school, but now I could hear nothing. In the house the shadows were turning to gloom so I went and lit the lamp. Pa was half-dozing on the chair. As I lit the lamp he raised his head, and he said, 'Oh, night already? How you feeling now, boy?'

'Fine, Pa. Good.'

'You eat yet?'

'Not yet. But I feel as if I could eat a lion.'

'We cooked the small one.'

I laughed.

'I never see a man to sleep like you.'

'Feeling revived now though.' I went again and looked out at the front door.

'Go and eat,' Pa said.

I did not say anything and my heart was thumping for as I looked out through the front door Rosalie Gidharee was standing right there in the road. Seeing me she smiled and walked away a little.

I said now, 'Pa, I'll come back in a minute eh.'

I went out into the road.

◆

When I got back into the house it was very late. My mother had already returned and was in bed. I sneaked in and seeing that Pa was not on the little bed I was relieved and I lay down there to sleep. Having slept all day sleep would not come to my eyes now and I kept thinking about Rosalie. I could not get her out of my mind. I lay face down, and my heart was thumping against the mattress. After a while I got up and crept softly to the cupboard and poured myself a huge drink of rum. I was hoping to knock myself out so I could get to sleep and forget. I was terrified as to what could happen. Both Rosalie and myself were stark staring mad. I asked myself why in the name of reason I was so crazy. My father had warned me about this thing. I was wild and furious with myself.

Then Joan came to mind. Just next week Joan was coming. I had told Joan so many nice things in letters and was writing to her every night! And now this. Hell, I thought. I felt like knocking my head against the partition.

And then I began to slide into a dizziness and slowly it became as though my mind was being transported. A wave of careless-feeling and pleasure began to engulf me. I knew I was growing drunk from the rum. I started remembering Rosalie now and thinking of her with ecstasy. I wrested myself from this thought and tried to clear my head by sitting up. I opened the door a little but the night was pitch-black. Suddenly my head seemed to reel and I was flat on my back again. It must have been shortly after this that the rum knocked me flat.

21

When old year's day came, I went to that place at the back of our house which we just called 'The Back'. I walked through the bit of scrubland behind the house and downhill to the ravine, and I crossed the ravine and went up the hill to where the big cinnamon tree was. There were a number of coconut trees around, some short and easy to climb, but I did not come here for waternuts now. This hill was covered with long grass that lay on the surface and was not prickly, and I had always liked to come and sit here.

From here, you could not see much of the village, for the trees, but looking towards the sea, there would be that cloudy fringe of coconut trees, and above it, a strip of the blue bay. At times you could see white foam running across the blue.

Now I thought of these things quite absently. I had come here because I could not bear to stay around the house while the hours crept on so slowly. I had never been as nervous as this before. Joan was just arriving at six this evening.

I had already written to let her know the position at home. She would have to sleep with my mother as we had no extra bed and no extra room. I had felt a little embarrassed about that but she had written back to say she did not mind one bit. It was as long ago as August that I had last seen her and I was quite anxious to see her again.

I was amazed that her mother had trusted us so much that she was allowing Joan to come for a few days. True, her mother had written to Ma about it, and it was all very official but I did not expect they'd be so brave. It was clear that they had a great deal of confidence in her. Much more than I had in myself.

The sun was filtering through the leaves of the coconut trees and making patterns on the ground. A great part of the slopes was in sun. At the foot of the slopes was a ridge of shadow cast by the bamboo patch. When we had first come to Pierre Hill I used to come here and sit on a coconut branch and slide down the slippery grass right down to the bottom to the edge of the bamboo patch. Even now I did this sometimes – although I was fifteen, and with hairs on my chest!

I sat with my knees drawn up to my chin and looked at the sun bright on the trees and on the grass. From here the bamboo patch looked dark and damp-looking, but on the top of it, the young, fine leaves were silvery in the sun. Here, under the cinnamon tree, the place was cool and heavily shadowed. Above the trees before and below me I could see only a few house-tops, and the atmosphere was very calm and I was thinking how beautiful everything was on this the last day of the year.

My shirt was unbuttoned and I was half-consciously playing with the hairs on my chest. Then I suddenly thought of Rosalie and I became a little frightened about her. Lately I had been thinking of Joan so much that I had almost forgotten what had happened. I tried to chase things from my mind now.

Six o'clock seemed as far away as eternity. It was only eleven now. Yet six would come. Soon it would be afternoon, and then evening. I began feeling nervous. Joan would soon be here. Even since I had sat here the sun had gone higher over the bamboo patch. Six o'clock would come all right.

I got up to stretch my legs and I was looking up into the cinnamon tree. This was a very unusual kind of tree, for the leaves were not green, but in many shades of brown and red, and its bark was rough and frayed and looking somewhat like Grenada spice. It had a strong, spicy smell, too.

I started looking towards the village. Pierre Hill proper was more bush than village from here, and there was not much to be seen. I looked across to the sea and there was the broad, blue strip in the distance, just on top of the green haze of palms.

'Green Mayaro,' I said to myself, and I wondered if Joan would like this place.

My heart was thumping for her.

22

My heart pounded as I watched Joan step out of the bus at the junction. As she got down I stretched out my hand to her, and taking, she leaned a cheek towards me and I did not know why I did not kiss it. She looked strangely grown and it was only as she rested down her grip that I noticed her high-heeled shoes.

'I'll carry the grip,' I said. 'How's things?'

'All right.' She was grinning.

'You looking so different, girl, O God.'

She only laughed.

She was looking so smart and fashionable that I felt foolish not having dressed up to meet her. At least I could have worn my new long pants. I thanked goodness, though, that my clothes were clean.

We waited while the cluster of passengers cleared away. The grip was rather heavy but I did not want to rest it on the ground so I changed hands.

'I'll help you with the grip,' Joan said.

'No, it's all right, it ain't heavy.'

We moved off. She looked towards Pierre Hill. 'This way?'

'Yes – we going right up that hill.'

There were a great number of people about the junction and as we walked along I became very self-conscious about Joan. By now most of the people here knew me and they kept looking at me and staring at Joan. I was feeling embarrassed, yet, in a way, proud to be seen with a girl like that. I knew I surprised a lot of people.

There were two points I wanted to pass by unnoticed. Firstly, Freddie's café – which was just ahead of me now. Freddie had known all about Joan's coming but I still did not want him to see me with her now. As we drew near the stone bridge outside the café, I said, 'Walk a little faster, Joan.'

She looked at me. 'Something happen?'

I laughed. 'No, it's just these fellers in the café here. They always keep on staring at new girls, you know.'

'Your new girls?'

'My new girls?' I laughed. 'I don't do that, girl. No, I mean any new face that pass across here. You know how boys is.'

'That's all right,' she said.

As we passed in front of the café I kept my head straight. There was the usual buzz of talking and when it was nearly behind us there came a sudden shrill whistle.

'Don't look,' I said.

Joan laughed. 'Boy, you so silly.'

I did not know whether it was Freddie who had whistled, or

any of the other boys, nor did I know if it was done because of us. Anyway we were clear of them now.

'It's great to see you, Joan.'

'Thanks. How you spent your Christmas – all right?'

'Yes. Very nice, girl. You?'

'Oh, we had a lovely time.'

'A royal time – like the queen?' I said and laughed.

Joan did not see the point.

'Girl, I was thinking about you all, all the time.'

'Oh yes?'

'No, I mean true, true. Perhaps you didn't even remember I was alive.'

'And what about all those letters?'

'But the point is you wasn't *thinking* of me all the time.'

'A little.'

'How much?'

'This much.' She showed a good deal, with her hands, so I felt good.

'I really glad they let you come.'

'Boy – '

'What?'

'No, it's all right.'

'They didn't want you to?'

'Mainly Pa. I had to make a row.'

'A *row*?'

'Oh, don't worry about that. Don't worry because if they didn't agree for me to come I still couldn't come, anyway.'

I was growing more and more excited about her. Just to hear her talk thrilled me. 'Oh, girl, you'll never know – I mean I'm so glad you made it.'

'I wanted to.'

'You is a wall. And you looking nice too bad – O God!'

'But I'll tell you one thing,' she said gravely. 'No monkey

business. That is what caused all the trouble. They trust me, but you know, only up to a point. So you see what I mean. You'd better know that from now.'

'What you really mean?'

'You know.'

'You don't trust me any?'

'No.'

I laughed, but Joan was quite serious.

'Now why you don't trust me, Joan?'

'You are a boy. Not true?'

I was a trifle disturbed and I said, 'I mean I know people does say that kinda thing but I don't really see why you should feel like that. You know, nobody seem to trust anybody.'

'Cheer up,' she smiled. 'I only said that just so.'

We were a little way up Pierre Hill. She was looking completely relaxed again and was looking around at the place. I had to rest the grip a bit now and she stood up with me and then we went on again. She was walking rather slowly in her high heels because of the softening pitch and as I walked on I wondered what the hell she had in this grip. Girls always took all their belongings with them wherever they were going. It was as if she was coming home to stay a year. I'd have loved that! I looked at her and she was looking at the roadside trees. Along the hill the golden-apple trees were in full leaf again, and there were damsel trees, too, with their clusters of cherries yellow in the sun. I hoped she found this pretty.

'Ever come up this hill before, Joan?'

'Not really.'

'Who you was spending this holiday at – I mean for Discovery, when you was here?'

'Sheila Maynard.'

'Oh, yes. I remember now. I ask you about this before – remember?'

'I remember but you forgot.'

'I have a bad memory. And yet I don't forget about you. Suppose you'll be going to see the Maynards?'

'But naturally! I must go and say hello. Why?'

'Nothing.'

She knew I was jealous. She was walking even more stylishly now beside me. As we neared the slight levelling-off of the hill I kept the Gidharees' house in mind. This was the second place I wanted to pass by unnoticed. I said, 'You lagging back, Joanie. Just step a little faster.'

'I'm on my last, boy. This hill is hell.'

'*What?*'

She laughed.

She had looked so charming and simple saying that, that I felt a gush of tenderness for her.

'All right, bear up. It's just a little way now.' I put my arm about her waist. Then there was someone coming in the distance and I let my arm slide down. We passed the Gidharees' house, with me keeping my head straight, and I hoped no one saw us. I glanced at Joan and of course she had no idea of Rosalie and she flashed me a smile.

Now she said, 'This is a cashew tree, isn't it?'

'Yes. They ain't have none in Sangre Grande?'

'I've never seen any there. But we used to have one in the school garden.'

'Oh we have lots here. This one had some nice rosy ones up to the other day. So you never eat a cashew?'

'I've had lots of cashew-nuts.'

I burst out laughing. 'I ask you if you ever eat a *cashew*, answer that.'

'No I never. What's so funny about that?'

I couldn't stop laughing, 'But you buy cashew-nuts in the shops?'

150

'Naturally.'

I laughed until we got right up to our house, and then I said, 'Okay, Joan, here is where we live girl. Okay?'

She looked nervous.

'Come on,' I said, 'they'll like you.'

Glancing back as I turned to go into the house, my heart jolted. Rosalie Gidharee was standing looking at us.

23

Now the next day – New Year's holiday – we did not go to the school fair. Somehow I had the feeling Rosalie would do something desperate so I changed my mind. Joan was very disappointed, for I had written telling her about the fair and she had looked forward to it. She had brought extra clothes especially for this. I had to make all sorts of silly excuses but she accepted them.

During the afternoon I took her down to that wonderland of bamboo and coconut trees at the slopes behind our house. I thought she might like some coconut water. These fields belonged to Gordon Grant but I used them freely. The scenery here was strange to Joan – for Sangre Grande did not have many coconut trees – and she was in love with it right away. I took her right up the grassy slope to the cinnamon tree, with the bamboo patch below us. Standing up under the cinnamon tree I pointed out the fringe of coconut palms at the sea-shore, and above the palms, that deep-blue fringe that was the sea.

'Goodness!' she gasped, 'how far is that from here?'

'I'll say about a mile. Perhaps.'

'This is *stupendous*,' she said.

I didn't know what that meant but I could see it meant something good because there was wonder in her face. The sun was filtering through the trees onto the slopes, and in front of me, on top of the bamboo patch, birds were pecking at the young leaves.

'Look at that.' I pointed to the bamboo patch.

She looked and at once she sighed. Then she said, 'Boy, this is great.'

'It's always like that here.'

'I like here,' she said.

'Let's sit down.'

She brushed the grass first, then sat down, smoothing her dress under her. 'Shell, this is wonderful. I like things like this. You?'

'Yes, I like here. I like Mayaro on the whole.'

'I wish I could write poetry. This sort of thing – you know I feel people should write poetry about this.'

She looked quite excited.

'Really?' I said.

'Yes, I feel so. I ever told you about Janet Chan?'

'No.'

'Well she's a Chinese-Creole friend of mine. You know, she is the secretary or something of this literary sort of club, *Music Belongs to the World*. It's mainly for classical music and so on, but they hold all kinds of meetings, and they read poetry there and all that. *She'd* like this.'

'Yes?'

I was thrilled to find Joan liking Mayaro so much. She was greatly moved. I was moved too but not that much.

She said, 'This girl, Chan. She could write good poetry, boy, oh Christ!'

'Well why she don't write them in a book then and get famous?'

She was taken aback by this. She thought for a while then she said, 'It's not so easy as all that.'

We were silent now and she seemed enrapt in her thoughts. I did not want to interrupt her. I looked at her quietly and after a moment I said, softly, 'Well, I'll climb for some waternuts now – okay?'

From wherever she was in spirit she came back to me. 'Okay,' she said, and smiled.

I had brought my bush cutlass with me and now I got up and stuck it into the ground and buckled my belt tighter. Then I began to look around for a lowish coconut tree with good nuts. I could have cut a pole and prodded down some waternuts, so short were some of the trees, but I wanted things a little more adventurous, to impress Joan. I did not want too tall a tree because these water nuts burst when you dropped them from a great height. Of course you could catch them – but I knew Joan would not try that. Now I spotted an ideal tree and I took up the cutlass.

'Come over here, Joanie.'

She got up from the slippery grass and I held her hand, tugging her to the flat ground above the slopes. She was wearing crepe-soled shoes, and as she walked they made little squeaking noises on the grass.

Her wear this morning was another smart-fitting dress, cream coloured, which made her look mild. Her hair was very prettily combed and this was one of the points that softened me with girls.

'You don't straighten your hair, Joan?'

'Never.'

'Great girl. I wish there was more like you.'

I put my hand on her hair – it was so inviting, and this led to my wanting to kiss her – but I did not want to start this yet.

We came to the foot of a tree that I was going to climb and I made her sit down a little way off. I lay onto the tree and climbed pretty fast and when I was half-way up I stopped for a rest and looked down at her. She laughed. She put a hand beside her mouth and said: 'You could climb like a squirrel, boy.' I laughed. I started climbing again and now I was among the waternuts.

Getting between two branches I looked down at her. She seemed a long way below. She was not looking up and I could see the profile of her head and down her beautiful neck and down the front of her dress, and I felt a strange tenderness towards her. I put two fingers under my tongue and whistled. She looked up. I called: 'What sort you like – hard jelly or soft, or pure water?'

She had both hands over her eyes for the sun, and looking up into the branches at last her eyes found me. 'You know, *mixed*, jelly and water,' she cried.

She looked confused and I laughed. She did not know much about coconuts. I picked some that were heavily jellied, and some lightly jellied, with lots of water. I picked about six and slid down from the tree.

Then I began peeling them. I peeled hers quite daintily, so she could drink without spilling the juice onto her dress. I said, 'Hold this careful. This juice does stain bad.'

'Okay.'

As she bent over to take it she caught my eyes lowered and I quickly pretended I was looking at her brooch. She said nothing but put the nut to her mouth.

I peeled my waternut by slashing it flat across the top then taking the point of the blade and making a hole in the hard shell. This way of peeling waternuts – cutting it flat across the top – we called *Chinese-face*, and now as I put the nut to my mouth I couldn't help chuckling.

I stopped drinking. 'Joan, this girl from the what-you-call-it again? – the Music something club—'

'*Music Belongs to the World*,' she said.

'Yes. That secretary girl, what's her name again?'

'Janet Chan.'

'Oh yes.'

'Why?'

'No – nothing.'

She looked round at me. 'If you asked a question like that there must be some reason.'

I burst out laughing.

She did not know why I was laughing but she began laughing too. 'Why – what about Janet?'

'No, nothing. I tell you it's nothing. It's really silly, really. You see I just peel my nut in *Chinese-face* and it make me remember this Chinese girl just like that.'

She giggled. '*Funny*,' she said.

I could not drink for laughing.

Joan said, 'She's a nice girl – Janet. And good-looking too. Boy, she's a serious girl. A brain, really.'

'You must introduce me. I'd like to know her.' I was teasing.

'Well go ahead,' she said. I could see she was having trouble to finish off the nut. Everytime she stopped drinking to talk she looked as though she would never make it. The coconuts on this hill were quite large and had lots of water. Now she leaned back trying to finish off the nut. Suddenly straightening she caught my lowered eyes again.

'I'll introduce you,' she said, and continued drinking.

'So you don't mind if I get to know Janet, eh?'

She drank rather slowly, swallowing 'gluck-gluck', and then she was finished. She looked across at me and said, 'No.'

155

'Good. I like that.'

She put down the nut beside her and I slashed it open in three parts and I cut her a 'spoon' to eat the jelly with. Her face was the smoothest black I had ever seen and in using the cutlass I had to take my mind off her or I might have cut myself. I started peeling another nut and she said, 'I can't drink no more you know. Sorry.'

'Okay. Cutting this one for me.'

'Chinee-face?' she said and broke into laughter.

'Ah, girl.'

'I'll tell Janet about you.'

After I had peeled the nut and was drinking she eased up close to me. 'You know you are a nice boy?'

'How come?'

'Don't know.'

'Hug me up.'

As she threw her arms about my neck it shook me and spilled some of the coconut water on my shirt. She did not see this and I did not say anything. I was brimming with tenderness for her.

'You are a *very* nice boy,' she said.

'But be careful.'

'No, I mean it.'

I rolled the nut away with half the water still inside. I turned and put both my arms about her and I said, '*You* is the sweetest jane in Trinidad.'

As I held her she seemed to freeze up and was as stiff as board, so I let her go again.

'Look, you'll treat me like that, won't you?' she said.

'What you mean?'

'Well, you said I'm a nice jane. I want you to treat me like that.' I held her again and again she stiffened. 'Joan, what's wrong?'

156

There was silence.

'You scared of me or something?'

'Yes.'

I laughed. 'Why?'

'Don't ask why. I'm just scared stiff, that's all.'

'You wouldn't kiss me?'

'If it would stop there – yes.'

I pulled her closer and for a few minutes she only let me kiss her cheeks and her eyes but she would not let me get to her mouth and I squeezed her to me and tried to find her mouth and we were soon over on the grass. Then she was still, and when she let me take her mouth, and kiss her as I liked, I felt so strange and maddened it was as if I wanted to devour her. Joan was blowing hard through her nostrils and I had my hand at the back of her neck and as I moved it round she grabbed it and wrung it. 'No!' she said, emphatically. After a moment she moved away her mouth. 'Stop now,' she said.

'What's wrong? You is my girl so what the hell!'

'I said to stop now.'

'O God, Joan.'

'What you think I am, boy! Listen, I still going to school you know, for Christ sake!'

I was furious. I leaned over staring at her. She lay with her head on the grass. She looked up at me weakly and I had the feeling she was helpless. There was silence for a while and then she said, 'Stop puffing like a silly old bull,' and she burst out laughing.

I didn't laugh, and she said, 'You is an old terror, boy.'

'Just a while ago you said I was *very* nice.'

'Yes, but then look how you was behaving.'

'I is only human. And I love you.'

'That's not love – that's real trouble, boy.'

I couldn't say anything.

'And don't forget *you* said I was the nicest jane in Trinidad. But you want to get me involved.'

'Not really. But I can't help it.'

'Well I'm afraid you'll have to help it, Mister. So that's why you invited me here? That's why you so wanted me to come to Mayaro for New Year's?'

'Trust you to talk like that.'

'It's true,' she said. '*True, true, true.*' Then she said, 'And he writes such innocent letters, you'll never think he's a maniac.'

'I ain't no maniac. I want you – that's all I know.'

'And by the hook or the crook, eh?'

'*You* saying that – not me.'

She lay silent now. Her head was on the grass and there was a bit of sun on her face. As she lay she had her feet together and her dress smoothed right down to her knees. She looked like Venus draped.

There was something I had wanted to say to her since she arrived at Mayaro but I had kept putting off saying it. I felt afraid even now, just in case she said no. But this was the best chance I had.

'Joan.'

She looked across at me.

'I'd like to get married to you.'

I expected her to be shocked because we had never spoken about this, but she just lay there silently and said nothing. My heart was thumping.

I said, 'If you agree – how long do you think we'll have to wait?'

'Four, five years, maybe,' she said calmly.

I was elated that at least she wanted us to get married.

'But four or five years is a long time, Joan. I can't wait that long.'

'Poor boy.'

'I'm suffering.'

'Poor old Shell. I wonder if that's what he tells every girl.'

'What make you say that.'

'Nothing – I just wondered.'

I could hardly take my eyes off her. She was looking up into the coconut trees again. But I could see she was thinking. Now she inclined her head towards me and she said, 'You really want to get married to me?'

'But of course, Joan. I mean you *know* that.'

'Well the fact is, we'll have to wait. But what I want to say is, Shell – I mean I have to be plain, all right? – What I want to say is, if anything happen to me – you know what I mean – you wouldn't just bail out on me?'

'No. O God, Joan, a thousand times no.'

'Because Daddy will kill me.'

I said nothing.

'Boys do that, you know. Boys do that sort of thing all the time. I even knew a girl who was like that. I mean, this is facts!' She sat up.

'Joan, O God, you know I'll never do that to you.'

'I've thought of all this before you know. Don't think I didn't think about this.' She began growing calmer and afterwards she was looking up at the sun in the coconut trees. Then she chuckled: 'Funny how we've got so involved. Considering I didn't even know you before Discovery.'

'Life funny, eh?'

I eased up close beside her and I put my arm round her neck. We did not speak. There were a few blades of grass in her hair and I plucked them out.

I said now, 'And what about you – you want us to get married?'

'Aha.'

'You think we'll get on all right? – Together, like?'

'Oh Christ, boy, I'm sure.'

'You always saying, "O Christ".'

'Sorry.'

'It's okay. I don't really mind. I mean I want to get married to you, bad. I only hope we wouldn't have to wait four whole years.'

'We may have to.'

'I don't know. But I'm sure we'll have to.'

I pulled her over on me and I was going to kiss her but she moved her head. She said, 'We'll have to wait two years at *least* – I bet.'

'Give me a kiss.'

There was no sound from her. I turned her face towards mine and this time she made no fuss. I kissed her and she threw both her arms around my neck.

'Let's move from here,' I said.

Here it was deserted as always, but if anyone chanced along we were in open view. We got up and I led her past some short coconut trees into a place that was cool, and shielded by tall wild ochroes. Then I sat on the grass and she lay over and rested her head on me and we talked.

When we got up from the grass we walked out to where we had picked the nuts but Joan did not want any more and I peeled one for myself. We had left two behind. I just drank the water, without cracking the nut for the jelly, and I gathered up all the shells and husks and threw them into the bush.

I said, 'When you thief, thief clean.'

She laughed.

I stuck the point of the cutlass into the waternut we had not used and dragged it along. Maybe my father would like it. Because of his illness there were so many things he could not have. He could eat lots of things but not drink. I was thinking of asking Joan what she thought of my father but just at that moment she spoke.

'Have a pen-knife?'

'No, why?'

'Just wanted to carve something on that tree. To remember.'

'Oh, that's nice. Come.'

We went up to the cinnamon tree. There was wire binding the handle of my cutlass to the blade. It was stiff wire and I unwound a bit of it and twisted this and snapped it off. I said, 'See if you could use this.' She leaned against the tree and on a smooth brown part of the wood she carefully etched: *Joan and Shellie New Years Day* – and beside this she was trying to inscribe the year. When she finished this she turned round giggling, 'Shellie, don't look at this little part.'

'Why not?'

'Just don't look now, but you must come back and see it when I'm gone back.'

I turned away, but glancing back slyly I saw that she was tracing a little heart. This amused me because it did not seem something to turn away for. Then she was writing something under the little heart. I went and stood up behind her and she embarrassedly buried her face in her hands. She had written, I LOVE YOU.

'Don't look!' she cried. 'Come on, now. Come on, let's go.'

I held her hands and she walked weakly down the hill.

24

New Year's day had passed since Wednesday and Joan was staying until Saturday. We had spent most of the time in the house talking. Joan liked talking to Pa. They talked about all sorts of things and sometimes they did not even bring me into the conversation. I often sat listening to them. However, today being Friday, Joan thought she'd better go over to see the Maynards, and at last Pa and I got together for a while. He called to me directly she left.

'So what you going to do with this Joan?'

I'd like to get engaged, and afterwards get married.'

'Get married when?'

'Two or three years' time.'

'You joking or what? Three years' time you'd be just over eighteen. That's much too young.'

I said nothing. I had definitely made up my mind but I was prepared to hear him out.

He was silent now, and then to try him out, I said, 'I'll give her about eight years, I think.'

This seemed to startle him. 'How old you say she is now?'

'Like me. Going in sixteen.'

'In eight years she'll be twenty-four. Somebody'll search her up long before then.'

'Well that will be all right.'

'You serious or you making joke?'

'Serious. Why not?'

'Well listen, if you don't like the girl stop playing the fool round her – you hear?'

'Well you say two or three years too young. What you want me to do? Well I'll give her ten years if you want.'

'Listen, boy. You just past fifteen now, you'll soon be twenty! Even twenty is young for marrieding, but I'll agree to twenty. If you two love each other – and if you ain't have too much *steam* – you could wait five years.'

'I can't wait five years.'

'All right. All right, you is a big man – you wearing long pants. Do what you like. I finish talking.'

I let a few moments pass for the tension to die away, then I said, 'You like her?'

'Yes. Oh yes. Yes, I think she's a very nice child.'

'Good.'

I thought of asking him how he felt about Rosalie Gidharee now, but I did not want to embarrass him. He went on: 'What I like about Joan is, she so simple, and yet she have a dam' good education, you know. She more educated than you.'

'Well I know. She going to a good school.'

'You is a dam' lucky feller. I glad for you, boy.'

'What about Ma – Ma like her?'

'But she was telling you – '

'Yes, but what I want to know is, what she tell *you*. I mean Ma wouldn't tell me everything.'

'Oh, that's what you think? When it come to a case like this your Ma ain't 'fraid to talk, boy. You could bet she wouldn't lie to you. At least I know she wouldn't sweet-talk you. We really like Joan. Your mother like the way she talk good English and thing. We like Joan a lot.'

'But you want me to wait five years.'

'Look, it's for your own good. I giving you advice as a father. The world ain't running away.'

'Look, Pa, people always saying the world ain't running away. People always saying things like that. I mean I like Joan and I don't know. I know the world ain't running away, but still. You see what I mean? I mean, Pa, you see the point?'

'Calm down,' he said. 'You getting yourself all confused.'

For the rest of that evening I was very glum. The only thing that cheered me up was my long pants. I had got my long pants for New Year's but I had not worn it as we had not gone anywhere. But this morning I had put it on to show them in the house, and I had kept them on, and now that Joan had returned I was going to take her out for a walk on the beach.

We left the house at about seven o'clock, when it was turning dusk. Joan was very proud of my long pants. She said I looked like a real man. She herself looked so elegant that I was most anxious that things should work out properly and that we would not have to wait five years. Somehow, although I was still shy about people looking at us, I wanted everybody to see us now and I held her hand as we walked. Glancing over at her I suddenly remembered New Year's day when I was looking down at her from the branches of the coconut tree and I said, 'Joan, I didn't know you used to wear *that* already?'

'What?'

I told her and she quickly slapped my face. 'That's for being fresh! I didn't even know you knew about those things.'

I laughed.

'You probably even had girls before!'

'Never.'

'Kiss the cross.'

I made a cross with my fingers and kissed it.

'All right,' she said.

We passed in front of Freddie's café as he was getting ready to light his gasoline lamp. His head was down and he was pumping and he did not see me. There were a lot of people in the café. I sincerely wanted Freddie to see me, especially as I was with Joan, and also I had not seen him since Christmas night and I wanted to call in and at least say 'Happy New Year,' to him. He was the sort of fellow who would appreciate this, and who would shake your hand and wish you back a happy New Year, and wish you God Bless and prosperity in all your undertakings. As I went by I was thinking of this, with Joan silent beside me.

Day-dreaming, I could almost feel Freddie's hand-shake and his gruff voice wishing me all the best and God speed. He was a man like that. Sometimes I liked sentiment and I liked warmth.

'You're well quiet,' Joan said.

This roused me. 'I was thinking about Fred.'

'Aha?'

'I like him. Funny.'

'You wanted to pass in there, I suppose.'

'Yes, really,' I said. 'I mean you meet so many people, and yet there's a few fellers who you meet and really like. I mean, take Freddie – Freddie is not an educated feller and all that – he'll talk about drinking, and hunting, and girls, and all that, all, all, the time – you know that sort of thing? – and yet he's such a good feller – I mean, this girl you was telling me about – this Carmen Chan – he'll appreciate a girl like that, although she's so educated and he isn't. And *she'll* appreciate him too. You see the point? Now this wouldn't happen with the other fellers. It's funny. Look, this Freddie have a picture there, over the ice-box, a picture called: *The Flotsam and Jetsam of the Sea*. Well, nothing in that, but you know, he like that sort of thing – funny, eh? – he's just one of those fellers I happen to like.'

'I understand what you mean. But I wasn't telling you about any Carmen Chan. It's Janet Chan, good Christ.' She was laughing.

'I know, all right, I know. But you see the point I want to make? He'll even appreciate you – I mean you talk good English and all that.'

'I talk good English?'

'Ma said so. Pa too. They like you a lot.'

'Well I don't talk good English, for your information.'

'All right, let's forget it. I was only telling you about Freddie.'

'But mind you, I'd like to.'

'Okay, okay.'

We were walking on the long-stretch on the other side of Station Hill, just past the Government School. The road was lined thickly with coconut palms. The darkness straight ahead – where the road ended – was the sea. That was about half a mile away. I was still thinking of Freddie, and also I was listening to the sea. Without concentrating on this, I could tell by the sound of the sea that the tide was out and that we would have a wide beach. I was pleased about this because I wanted Joan to see how wide the beach could get. There was still Freddie in my mind and I wanted to stop thinking about him a little and chat to Joan. I had heard her voice a while ago, and now, coming back from far away, I said, 'What's that you was saying, Joanie?'

'Nothing. People talking to you and you dreaming away!'

'Sorry. Let's hear you again.'

'Who? Not me.'

'Oh, Joan. Why you so fussy this evening? Let's hear you.'

'I don't talk twice.'

'Oh come on, man, Joan. Talk about something. Tell me about old Charmayne and Jake, and old Zay and Zita, and all that.'

'We talked about all that last night.'

'Let's talk about it again, man. I could never get tired of hearing about your family, girl. They kill me.'

She said nothing for a while, and then she said, 'One thing I can't stand is to be talking to people while they're dreaming away there on me.'

'Good Christ, Joan, you still with that?'

'Don't keep on saying "Christ".'

The dusk was very heavy now. After walking in silence a little I brought her to a stop and I said, 'Forget the little quarrel, eh? The old thoughts was far when you was talking. Sorry. Life so funny. I don't know why I should be so taken up with Freddie all of a sudden.'

I twined her arm about my waist and mine was about hers. We started walking again. She said, 'I suppose it's because you ain't have no brothers, that's why.'

We walked on in silence. We were near the beach now and the sound of the sea had risen. Before us, on either side, were the lights of Plaisance. We watched the lights of the houses through the coconut trees. There was the sound of the little waves breaking and running up the sands. The tide was definitely right out. Apart from the noise of the sea, there was complete silence.

'Now *you* well quiet,' I said.

She smiled. Her teeth sparkled in the darkness.

Getting onto the beach we turned left and walked towards the flood gates and towards the beach-house, *Ocean Star*, and I showed this to Joan because that was where my mother worked. At *Ocean Star* we turned back and walked towards the little place called Lagon Mahoe and then, passing here, we went on towards St Ann. St Ann was where the RC school was, and farther down was Radix, where we used to live. That was the place we nicknamed 'Down-the-Beach'. Joan knew all about these things from my letters but I did not mention them now. The night was black now and there were many stars over the sea. As we walked on, Joan was pulling me further and further towards the water. We walked on and hardly spoke.

After some time Joan said, 'It's funny how all here feels so familiar.'

'Oh yes?'

'I think it's those letters of yours. You told me so much about Mayaro.'

'It's silly, really.'

'No, I like that. I like letters like that.'

'This is the only place I really know. So I keep on talking about it.'

'That's all right. It's a nice place.' Then she giggled teasingly, 'Only a lot of mosquitoes.'

'Goodness – they give you hell?'

'Not much. Don't mention that to you Ma, please.'

'Okay. But sorry about that.'

'It's nothing. Forget it.'

'I get so used to them, meself, I don't even feel them now.'

She chuckled. Then she said, 'What a pretty beach, eh?'

'If it was daytime I'd show you all those boat-houses up there.'

'Show me? Don't forget I was on this beach before.'

'Oh yes – for Discovery – that's right.'

'We went up that flood gate. Then we walked this way down to a river.'

'That would be Lagon Mahoe. Just after that is St Ann, where the RC school is.'

'How far is that from here?'

'About a mile again.'

She said nothing.

'You want to see it?'

'Not really. We can't see anything in this darkness.'

She was holding me tighter now. We were right down on the water's edge and every now and again we had to scamper away from the little waves.

I said, 'What you want to do – just walk, or turn back?'

'Let's find some place to sit down.'

We began to squeeze each other until we came to a stop.

'Joanie.'

'Let's find some place to sit down – and kiss.' She burst out laughing at her own daring.

'You trust me so much now?'

'Yes, because I know you'll be a good boy.'

'I'll be a very good boy,' I said.

'Yes, Shell. Let's find some place and sit down.'

'Yes, and I'll be good, eh? I'll be good this time'

'Yes, but don't be too good.'

We laughed in the darkness.

25

The New Year had well set in and now with Joan gone a long while, and with Pa back at the Colonial Hospital, life took on a new hopelessness and a new pain. My father had given me a good talking to before he left. He did not want me to go back to work in the cocoa. More so because he was highly impressed with Joan, who was so cultured – according to him – and who spoke such good English. (For him, speaking good English was something big.) He did not want me to go back to the cocoa field but he could not suggest what I should do. He talked about my trying to get back in to school and seeing if I could do the *First Year* teachers' exams, but that was impossible – I was already fifteen and they would not take me back. He despaired.

Even Joan he saw as a problem. He felt I could never be truly happy if I married her. Pa was wise, yet sometimes he said things which astonished me. He felt no man could be happy with a partner who was the more intelligent. He felt the husband should be superior in every way. I had not thought deeply on this but it did not seem to matter in the least who was the more intelligent. And in any case working in the cocoa didn't mean you were a damn fool.

The funny thing was, Joan had never mentioned the cocoa to me – except once, when she wanted to know what the hell was going on between Sonia and me. She soon saw it was innocent, and it became a joke, and then she forgot about it. She did not even ask about my future or any such thing. She just accepted me as I was.

Mind, Pa's argument did make me think a bit. It did make me feel that maybe if Joan found a successful man, with a good job, and who spoke as good English as she did, she would go to him. I did think this but it looked very unlikely to me, knowing Joan so well. But it worried Pa, though. It worried him too because we were equal in age and he felt that the man should be superior here too. He said every man should be at least two or three years older than his wife. I said, O God, Pa, it's not as if she's *older* than me! I know, he said – but he was not pleased. But this question did not worry me at all.

What worried me all the time Pa had been talking was his own health. And what made me really afraid was the manner in which he was talking – as if he didn't expect to come back. The fine, healthful look he had gained over the holidays had proved false. Even while Joan was still here I had begun to notice the falling away. There had been the quickening of breath, the difficulty in talking, the rasping of his chest in the night, and worst sign of all, the growing heaviness of cheek. By the Saturday he was due to leave the fluid had gathered so much in his belly, he could hardly stand.

My mother, always having premonitions and dreams, had been very fearful. Pa tried to pretend he was not feeling too badly, and not having too much pain, but she knew the truth.

She was very sore with me for the very little things which might have helped Pa on the way to this. She was sore about my drinking with him on New Year's day and for having brought him the water-nut, and for letting Joan make him stay up late. My father said this was all nonsense, and that he had been hell bent to enjoy this Christmas anyway, for who knew who would see another one? And he had whispered to Ma that she knew very well there was no hopes for what he had. In the same breath he asked her to keep courage, but she covered her face with her dress and went into the bedroom.

Having overheard him say that, it was as if a storm had struck me. In all my years it was the first time I had allowed myself to break down so completely, with my tears like falling rain.

That day was a very bad day for all of us, for Pa could not console us, and this pained him. He was very angry with me, in particular. He said, Buck up now, and pull your socks up! He said that I was looking for a wife but I could not even comfort my own mother. He used words like needles.

However, in the evening he tried to be bright and cheerful. He started talking with me about Port-of-Spain. He said, What a funny name, Port-of-*Spain* – why not Port-of-*Trinidad*? I said well it used to be a port of Spain, let's face it. He said oh yes, he knew that, but it wasn't so now, so why keep the 'Spain' in? I thought he had a point there but I wasn't sure. Then we launched into a little 'Battling' – that was what we called asking each other questions. Only I let him do all the questioning. He asked me who founded Port-of-Spain, and I said 'De Berrio,' right away.

'Try again,' he said.

'Don Jose Antonio de Berrio,' I said, almost arrogantly.

'Try again,' he said. 'Now you is a boy who just left school.'

I thought and thought, and it was so obviously de Berrio, that

I gave up, and I said, 'Well who was it then?' Then suddenly, as his mouth opened to tell me I cried 'Chacon,' and saved the points. We both had a good laugh. He asked me a few more questions and I answered them and he called to my mother: 'Evelyn, girl, this boy sharp too bad.'

She had been quiet in the bedroom.

Whenever my father and I discussed anything to do with education she was always quiet and listening. She liked to think I was intelligent. The evening passed off in this way, bittersweet, with the sweetness and laughter being very little, and the bitterness very full. For my father was to leave the next day and there was a great heaviness in the house. I went out into the street once only, and that down to the shops to buy fish. The conches of the fishermen had been sounding all afternoon and now as evening closed and the fish would be cheaper my mother sent me out. She made supper, but only Pa ate well, and at lamplight we were all ready for bed. Then Ma asked my father if he would pray with us. He was sleeping on the settee as he was again too ill for the bed. We brought him to the bedroom to pray. At first we said the twenty-third psalm together. Then Ma asked God quite openly if he would not preserve my father, and why. She said these doctors told her water under the heart was incurable, but she knew nothing was incurable with Him. She claimed that Pa was no burden at all whatsoever and that she was prepared to work for even a hundred years to look after him, once He left Pa to her. Then she was overcome and began to sob and she asked me to pray.

We were all three kneeling before the bed, with a candle burning, and I started to address God personally. All the time I prayed my mother cried. Then I too was overcome and could speak no more.

And quietly out of the darkness came the deep tones of my father's voice. He told God that he talked and talked to us but we would not hear. He said he loved home deeply and he loved us deeply, but since the Lord giveth and taketh away, blessed be the Name of the Lord. He said he could not fly in God's face, and even so, a man that was born from a woman had but a short time to live. He said he thanked God for letting him see his son grow up so big.

Then he prayed for my mother and for me and he asked God to preserve us. He was speaking to God so intimately, it was as if they had met and were friends. He said what he wanted for me – and he was asking this as a favour – was a good woman. If Joan was that woman, then let her light shine, so we could all see it. He said he was lucky with Evelyn and he had the feeling that the boy would be lucky too. He said if Evelyn and the boy would be happy he couldn't ask for anything else.

And after thanking God for the many little blessings, and for the Christmas, and for the light of the New Year, he said, 'Thy Will be done,' and we answered, 'Amen,' and we got up, and Ma went out with Pa to the settee and I heard her saying that she felt lighter. She came back to me within and she asked me to sleep alone on the bed tonight, and she got out some bedding, and she said she was going to sleep out in the sitting room, to watch with Pa. She whispered to me that if anything went very wrong we must try and not take it too hard – for that was life. If it was true there was a hereafter, she said, we knew where Pa would be – in Paradise. So we must be thankful. She rested her hand on my head a little, and then she left me. Afterwards I blew out the candle and lay in the darkness, and for me this was the most sombre night in the world.

26

The four dogs of Mr Gidharee and the host of strays shattered the peace of Pierre Hill. As soon as I heard them my heart leaped and I pushed the writing pad away from me, and I got up and went and stood up in the kitchen. I took up the cutlass from the corner and I stood listening to the movement of the dogs. The barking seemed to remain stationary outside our house and I knew that Mr Gidharee had not forgotten but was waiting for me. I slowly walked up the back steps and walked out to the front.

Now, being March, the sun was at its fiercest, and it had scorched the leaves off the lime tree, leaving a clear view from the road. As soon as I appeared at the door Mr Gidharee said, 'Come on, man, Shell, what wrong with you, eh – you keeping a man waiting.'

'Coming,' I said.

I went back within to shut up the house. I was feeling very fearful but I tried to tell myself things would be all right. Yet I had the feeling that I was taking a big risk to go into Cedar Grove today.

I put the writing pad and pen away on the shelf. I had just been writing to Joan to take things off my mind. Joan did not know of Rosalie and I certainly did not intend making her wise. Since Rosalie had seen Joan with me during the New Year's holiday, things had gone really badly, and she had threatened to tell her father that I had fooled around with her on Boxing night. I did not think she would dare, but I saw signs that made me feel she must have told him. Only yesterday I had seen them talking in the road and looking towards me. I had gone into the house very hurriedly, then. I had tried to avoid coming face to face with Mr Gidharee but a few days before he had come and knocked and asked me if I would go to Cedar Grove with him on Friday. I had been taken so unawares I could not make any excuses. Now, being Friday, from the time I got up I was uneasy.

I went out into the road now, and Mr Gidharee seemed cheery and bright. 'Hurry up, man,' he said, 'it getting late too bad.'

I smiled, but I was very nervous inside.

I had not seen the dogs for a little while. They looked more powerful and restless than I had known them, and they seemed so much on edge that I had to be a bit careful of them.

'Giving them dragon blood now,' Mr Gidharee said to me.

'What's dragon blood?'

'Oh that's something from the drug-store. To make them fierce. They too dam' lazy.'

We were going off up the hill and I was trying to drive the stray dogs away. Mr Gidharee's dogs were particularly vicious this morning and we had to struggle to keep them off the strays, and whenever I clapped or shouted after the strays the awesome barking of these four seemed to drown all the other noises of the village. At length we got the strays away. Rover, the black-and-white one, which I thought to be my friend, was exceptionally cross today, and when Mr Gidharee gave me his lead I avoided him as much as possible.

'With dragon blood,' Mr Gidharee said, 'they'll tear up their own mother to pieces.'

I walked beside the dogs uneasily. We had reached the crest of the hill now and were approaching the decline towards Spring Flat. We were walking on in silence and then Mr Gidharee said, 'But Shell, these days you scarce like good gold, boy.'

'I was working in the cocoa.'

'You so dam' scarce. I ain't see you since Christmas.'

A chill ran through me. Mr Gidharee had seen me only a few days ago when he had come to ask me to go to Cedar Grove with him. I wondered whether he had forgotten this or whether he had just wanted to mention Christmas. I said nothing.

'How you old man?'

'Very bad. He's worse now.'

'O God!' he said. He looked at me. He seemed to feel genuine sorrow.

We were silent for a while. My thoughts fled to Port-of-Spain. I wondered how was Pa today. Things had been going badly on that side too. Very badly. In fact, when I was writing to Joan this morning, it was to tell her I was intending to go up to Port-of-Spain soon. Mr Gidharee broke through my thoughts.

'So you in longs for good, then, Shell boy?'

'Almost.'

I did not feel thrilled about wearing long trousers now. In this depressed state of mind the novelty of this had worn off completely.

Mr Gidharee was looking me over. I was wearing a new pair of blue-dock trousers. Apart from the fact that my legs had grown much longer during these last few months, the long trousers were good for the bush, as a foil against prickles, and stinging flies.

'You looking good,' he said. 'You grow like hell, man.'

'Yes.'

I was trying to look cheerful and to be cheerful. For it had begun to occur to me that Mr Gidharee was just as usual and that it was my bad conscience that kept making me feel that things were different.

We walked on along Spring Flat and I was still very wary of the dogs. Tiger, the spotted one, kept growling and frisking about and this seemed to keep the rest in constant excitement. Rover, the black-and-white one, was surging on ahead and it was hard work for me to check him. Even the brown dog, Lion, usually so calm, was uneasy, and nervous-looking, and Hitler, the shining black one tugged at his lead, his nose to the ground.

I was so relieved when we got to Cedar Grove and Mr Gidharee released them. They fled up the road and into the bushes.

'That dragon blood will make them hunt like a bitch,' Mr Gidharee said gloatingly. It made me squirm. I did not like seeing the dogs in this state.

'You think this drug thing any good for them?' I said.

'Yes,' he said. 'Yes, of course. Very good for them. And adding me own little mixture.'

I was beginning to be aware of a strangeness in him. Maybe it was my own fearfulness that was making me think like this. But I thought I could see an inner heat and violence in his eyes. But I did not know. I was walking slightly behind him, and looking at him I could see how I had shot up past him, for I could see the top of his greying head, with the roots white as silver. Round his waist he had on that broad leathern belt, from which hung his cutlass, and he too was wearing blue-dock trousers and he was wearing a khaki shirt, stained with sweat under the armpits. On his feet were tyre-soled sandals, like the ones on my feet, and these were very good for the prickles – I could vouch for that. On the gravel of the Cedar Grove they made your walk soft and springy.

I watched Mr Gidharee walking in front of me and it was still doubtful whether Rosalie had talked or not. I hoped to God she hadn't. Although there seemed to be some more grey in that pile of wispy hair, as Mr Gidharee walked on with those, long, jerky strides, he looked younger and more agile than ever.

'You falling back, man. Come on.' He looked round for me. 'What you thinking about so much?'

I walked up beside him. The Cedar Grove was quieter now than when I was here last, but there were many birds in the trees, and there was screeching from the forest beyond. The sun of the dry season had scorched the trees and many of them were brown and shorn of leaf, and there was a lot more sky now between the branches. There were a great many dead leaves in the road.

From a distance I could see distinctly the path we would turn into, and as I was looking at this I heard a sudden noise and I cried, 'O God!'

It was Tiger who had sprung from the bushes. Mr Gidharee turned round and laughed. 'What happen?'

'Tiger make me jump.'

Mr Gidharee held his waist and laughed. 'Well, a big man like you get frighten for a little dog! Jesu Christ!'

My heart was still thumping. Tiger was running up the road now, his tail curled high above his back, his red tongue sticking out from the side of his mouth.

Mr Gidharee laughingly said, 'Anybody who you see get frighten easy have a guilty mind.'

This set the blood pounding inside me. He stopped all of a sudden and even this made me jump. He was pointing up into an immortelle tree. 'Look!' he said. 'What you think that is, up there?'

I did not see what he was pointing at and I said, 'Don't know.'

'Big hell of a wood-pecker!' he said.

I did not see it. He stood a little while looking up at the bird, and then we went on again.

As we turned into the track, first Rover, then Hitler, leaped out of the bushes. Both times I could not keep myself from

178

jumping, and my heart thumped voom-voom, and Mr Gidharee noticed how nervous I was, and I felt horrible and sick. Then I began making an effort to quieten down.

We came to the boundary flowers, and now, just a little way ahead, was the river. The boundary flowers looked thick and thriving in spite of the sun. Most of the small trees were scorched and the grass itself was very brown. Except where the new rice was sown, and where the earth looked brown and moist, everywhere the ground was crisp, but the crop did not seem to suffer from the heat. The potato beds were a great entanglement of vines, but had few leaves, and beyond this part – towards the fruit trees side – there was no more thick bush and I could see very clearly the cassava and the young corn.

'You see how the place is now?' Mr Gidharee said.

'Yes.'

The sun was already high and shining hotly, and there seemed to be vapour rising from the river and from the water-grass on the far bank. Perhaps it was just the mist clearing away. Wide, lazy Ortoire looked yellow-brown. It was easing along dreamily, carrying with it bits of dead leaves, and green leaves, and broken branches, and pieces of wood and bramble, and white frothy things that looked like frogs' spawn. For a moment I forgot Mr Gidharee and my nervousness with the dogs. I looked at the great water as it moved slowly by. Then I heard a crash and nearly fainted with fright.

'Tiger! You dam' silly idle coon!' Mr Gidharee shouted. Still shaking, I turned round. Mr Gidharee seemed more amused than annoyed with the dog. Then he glanced across at me and saw how I was. I was alarmed at the way things had gone this morning. I just could not control myself. Mr Gidharee did not say anything to me this time. We went on towards the shed, and he was looking at some sugar-cane shoots as he walked by. We came under the fruit trees and I did not even look up into them.

When we came to the entrance of the hut, Mr Gidharee said to me, 'Don't drop dead, you know, but Rover in here.' We went in.

The work Mr Gidharee had set out for today was to clean the weeds from the rice. We worked for a long while without talking and with the sun very hot. This was not like other times and I could feel this sharply. I knew something had happened, but whether it had to do with Rosalie or not I could not say. Mr Gidharee did not say anything unkind now but I could feel wrath in the air.

When my back was tired I stood up a little and I watched the river. Counting black stumps sticking out of the water, I told myself that I counted twelve alligators. I was trying to make fun with myself so I would cheer up. But one of the stumps disappeared, not far from the very bank, and I turned quickly to Mr Gidharee.

'Alligator! Just saw something sink down in the water. Just over there!' I pointed to the place.

'This place full with alligators,' he said. 'When I say full I mean *full*. If you just fall in there they'll tear you to shreds. Don't worry, man.'

I bent down again to pull weeds from the rice. It made me go all strange inside to think of what would happen if someone accidentally fell into that water. I'd make sure it wasn't me. I could just picture the alligators converging on the body and devouring the flesh, with blood oozing from the sides of their snouts. My heart was beginning to thump again. I eased a little further from the bank, into the rice-field.

After what seemed a long silence, Mr Gidharee said, 'How you like working in the cocoa?'

'Not too bad, for the time being.'

'Cocoa have plenty money in it he said. 'That is, if you *own* the blinking cocoa field.' Then he stood up, 'You see that piece

180

of cocoa land over there – that bit coming down like that, where my land finish?'

He was pointing to a stretch of cocoa-field that came down from the high woods to the river, just beyond his fruit trees.

'Yes.'

'I buying that so-and-so. The whole hog – land, cocoa, everything. Making arrangements.'

'O yes?' It came as a shock to me. I would have never thought he could afford that.

'I believe in land, boy,' he said. 'I believe in land and planting.'

I stood there amazed.

Mr Gidharee bent down to the rice again. 'That girl, Sonia, she does work with you?'

'Yes.' I looked up. I was very surprised at this question. I did not even know he knew Sonia.

'She's a nice, *good* girl.'

'Yes.' My heart began racing again.

'That is Ramdat daughter, you know. He like her too bad. He does make me laugh – this Ramdat. He say if any man play the fool round Sonia he'll *have* to married she, else he'll chop him up in fine pieces.'

A shudder ran through me.

Mr Gidharee went on: 'I agree with him. I mean to say if the man fool round the girl and then get married, that's okay, not so? Nobody wouldn't worry about that.'

I said nothing.

He said, 'You know, it's funny, but I like *Creole* people – I mean, you see my Marie. From a little boy I like *Creole* people. Especially decent *Creole* – like you. And I mean we is all the same people – *Creole* and Indian. But one thing about *Creole*, boy,' he stuck his cutlass violently into the ground, 'One thing with *Creole*, they like to play round but they don't like to get married. Never! Never!'

181

My hands were trembling as I rooted the weeds. I could feel the blood pounding in my chest.

'They prefer to get married to somebody else,' he went on. 'That does always happen. Because they feel the girl ain't good enough for them. Although she was good enough to play round with. This does hurt me. No wonder people does chop people for this sort of thing!'

He unstuck his cutlass from the ground now and wiped the earth from the gleaming blade. Then he took out a dirty handkerchief and wiped sweat from his face.

I was half on my knees and half-stooping. I was feeling desperate. My head was half-turned towards the river but I was keeping Mr Gidharee in view. I was not very close to him and if he only moved I'd break away through the bushes. Even the silence, now, terrified me and I wondered if I should break for the bushes now. My whole body was shaking.

'You can't blame old Ramdat,' Mr Gidharee said.

He began chopping again at the little weeds between the rice and he was doing so harder than before. I began working again too, but keeping him in view. As I tried to chop out the weeds I was so nervous I was chopping down the young rice.

'You had a good time over the holidays, Shell?'

'Yes,' I said. He had turned round to look at me and the eyes were penetrating, and the big nose and full lips confronted me. Then he seemed to relax.

'What happen, boy? You shivering like a leaf. It cold? Christ, the sun hot as hell, boy!'

I said nothing. I tried to carry on with the weeds and I was glad he could not see what I was doing to the rice.

'Get up, man, Shell. Let's go and eat something.'

He got up and led the way to the hut.

Oddly enough, he seemed quite normal now, and not as

terrifying as he had been a while ago. He got out roti and he gave me a whole one with salt-fish inside. Then he put the dogs' pans out of their reach and he put pieces of roti in each pan. I sat down on the plank in the shed with him standing beside me, and my nervousness had simmered down greatly, and I ate the roti and salt-fish, which tasted very good. From under the plank came the smell of ripe sapodillas, but looking underneath I saw there was nothing there. It was the smell that had remained from last year. The plank was very low and my legs felt cramped, so I stood up. Just as I stood up I saw Mr Gidharee was sprinkling some red powder from a packet into the dogs' pans. He turned his back to me. On the packet I had glimpsed the picture of two red fangs, and the words, 'Dragon's blood'.

After we had eaten and after the dogs had been fed, Mr Gidharee went out under the fruit trees close by. I went and kept close to him because the dogs looked very vicious, and were whining and yapping all the time. We were standing under the same orange tree I had climbed for him but I was not thinking of this very much for I was growing terrified of the dogs. Not knowing what to do I looked up at the sky because Mr Gidharee was doing the same. The air was warm and there was a large saffron-coloured cloud hanging over the river. There was no rustling in the trees.

'Rain will fall,' Mr Gidharee said.

He said it a little distantly and he seemed rather cool towards me again and rather remote from me. The sun was half-clouded and half-shining and though it was morning there was the feeling that noon was past. I was thinking all this and at the same time I was getting to my wits' end because of the barking and snarling of the dogs.

'Going to watch that piece of cocoa. Stay here a minute.'

Rover was lying under the orange tree, his head resting

sideways on the ground and he was barking. Tiger, too, was barking. He was barking at everything, and at moments he was barking at me.

I heard a plaintive yelping and I looked round. Hitler, the black one, was against a banana tree, with a hind leg propped against it, and he was apparently trying to pass water and finding much pain. Hearing him yelp like that really alarmed me. Lion, I did not see.

I looked round but Mr Gidharee had already disappeared. Beads of perspiration were rolling down my face. Tiger was still yelping and now the water was trickling from him. The barking of the other dogs rose now, and getting desperate, I cried, 'Mr Gidharee!'

The noise roused Rover into frenzy.

'Quiet, for *God* sake!' I waved my hand at him.

He lunged at me. I jumped back against the orange tree and picked up a broken bottle. I wanted a stick. Rover was snarling and drawing nearer. In desperation, I scraped my hand on the ground for a block of wood or something but there was only dust in my hand.

When Rover had rushed me Tiger sprang up and now they both lunged at me against the orange tree. I was frantic and wild. I threw out kicks and cuffs to keep them away, and I feinted them with a broken bottle, but still they kept coming. Now Tiger sprang straight at me and I rushed him with a kick and both he and Rover fled a little distance and in that brief space I broke a cassava tree with one snap to get the stick, and as Rover came in to me again I let him have one full blow across the head with the cassava stick, and he whined and fled, but Tiger became even more ferocious and was getting set to spring. I wanted another cassava stick as I had broken the last one on Rover's head. I picked up a handful of dust to throw at Tiger to keep him away, but as I rose Rover was rushing in and I side-stepped and fired a kick at him and missed but he went sprawling into the bushes. Tiger had not sprung yet and I made a rush at him and at the same moment he sprang and I managed to partly move away and he crashed into the orange tree. Now as I wheeled round to break a cassava stick I saw Hitler. Hitler was edging towards me, his teeth bared, and I made a few steps backwards. My shirt was wet with perspiration and my face felt bathed in it. I could not move back anymore because of the bush and as I tried to grab a handful of dirt, Hitler was on me and I could feel another dog about my legs. Punching and kicking at them I caught Hitler with a blow under the belly and he wailed and retreated. The other two dogs seemed all about me and I felt pricks as of needles and I did not know if these were from the razor teeth sinking in my flesh. With my flailing arms I managed to keep them off a little but there was no time to look round for a stick. Tiger rushed me again and I brought down a punch on his eye and this felled him just there before me. This seemed to get the other two even more ferocious and as Rover sprang at me I tried to side-step and fire a kick and the kick missed and there was a sudden pain on my knee-cap and as Rover tumbled in the bush he had the knee part of my trousers in his mouth. I was puffing and blowing but these dogs were not tiring but kept coming at me. I moved away from the orange tree to be in the open so I could see them from all directions. I felt liquid running down both my legs and I did not know if it was blood or sweat. There was no time to look for Tiger was snarling and getting ready to spring again. I backed away. Before he could spring Hitler rushed me from the side and I hit him so hard with my fist I felt a pain shoot up into my arm. I was panicking now. I looked round but there was no place to run. If I ran and fell the dogs would tear me up. The three dogs were advancing on me again and I backed away still more and now I was among the sweet-potato beds. All three rushed me here and I beat them off frantically with fists and elbows and I was kicking and shouting at them. My trousers were soaked and I did not even know when I had wet myself. Tiger, who was springing at me most, was drawing within range now and I moved back, then suddenly rushed in with a hammering fist on his head and I turned round to find Rover flying at me and then both of us went rolling over a potato bed. Now all three dogs were over me and I screamed out and lashed out with both hands and feet and there was the shrill whine of one of them and rolling over quickly I was on my feet again. Now, spotting the river close behind me I rushed furiously at the dogs and I let sing the broken bottle which I had forgotten in my left hand. As it missed, Hitler was upon me and I drove him back with a lump of forked-up dirt, and as he came in a second time I fetched him a blow with my heavy tyre-soled sandals and he fled whining. Snatching off one of my sandals I hammered Rover coming in. He got a heavy blow on the jaw but he still kept edging up. Then I heard a snarl from behind, and feinting with the sandal at Rover I swung a backhand blow at the dog behind me and I missed and the sandal slipped free from my hand. I grabbed a cassava tree and then and at the same time I felt one of the dogs' jaws round my leg and I turned round and rained blows wildly until the dogs retreated and the cassava tree was a stump in my hand. All three dogs were still preparing to jump at me and being on a potato bed I snatched handfuls of the loose, forked-up earth and I managed to keep them away with these. It was only now that I noticed blood streaming down my arms and my sleeves in tatters. Perspiration and blood were flowing down my legs and there was blood all over the dogs. Suddenly there came a rush from the bush beside the young rice and it was the brown dog, Lion, and I was just in time to bring him down with a fist in his mouth. We both fell down and immediately the other dogs were on me and I yelled out with all my might.

'What the hell going on here,' Mr Gidharee's voice said. 'What wrong with these blasted dogs! Come on here, Rover. *Rover*! Come on here, you buggers!'

The dogs left off all of a sudden, and went to him. Rover was limping. I had kicked him between his right hind leg and his testicles and the place was already swollen and he looked in great pain. Lion, too, was very shaken. I had hit him in his mouth with my fist and now both his mouth and my fist were streaming blood. I hobbled around and I found my sandal. I stood there panting, my blue-dock pants ripped all over and my shirt in strings. I was mainly in my underwear. I did not feel myself crying but my face was wet with tears. Perspiration was flooding down from my brows and from my arm-pits. My whole body seemed washed with it.

Mr Gidharee came and stood up beside me. 'What wrong with you and those stupid buggers?'

As I tried to answer I bit my lip for I felt I would break down. I was panting so heavily I had to hold my waist. My knees felt so weak with fatigue that as I tried to move I just slumped down on a potato bed.

Mr Gidharee said: 'Perhaps they know something about Rosalie. Perhaps that's why. Dogs does know things, you know. Perhaps they mean to tear you up unless you mean to get married to her. Dogs funny, boy.'

Then he turned round at the dogs, 'Look what you bitches do to my garden. Look at the rice! Look at the potato vine! You blasted lot of who-cut-your-head!'

As he stopped talking there was complete silence, for the dogs were quiet now. I did not look around for them. As I sat there with the breeze around me and my body growing cool I began to feel sharp, searing pains all over my body, and it was only now that I realised how much I had been bitten. Mr Gidharee turned to the dogs again: 'Come on. Not doing any more blasted work today. Everybody get up. We going home.'

It may have been about two or three hours afterwards when I suddenly became aware of myself still sitting on the potato bed. There was the murmur of the rain in the trees and a few stray drops sprinkled me. As I looked up, the sky was shimmering with light raindrops, and was very overcast. I felt quite unable and unwilling to get up. My head felt blank and it seemed I had awakened from a semi-sleep. There was a rumble of thunder and twice lightning brightened the darkening trees. There was a dull glow on the river, and the water looked as sluggish as oil. I could not guess what time it was but I presently heard noises that sounded as though the parakeets were going home. I sat there, and as I tried to move my legs I cried out for pain. Then my head began feeling numb. Then the clouds broke and water poured all over me.

27

A little time afterwards a telegram came to us. I heard my mother say, 'Jesus!' though I knew she could not have read the telegram yet. I was in the bedroom. I had been bed-ridden for two weeks, but I was aware enough now of what was going on about me to feel some alarm. My mother came straight into the bedroom. She said, 'O God something from the hospital.'

Her hands were shaking so much she could not open the little brown envelope. I took it from her. My head felt hot and I was perspiring as much from the fever as from the fear of what the message might say. I ripped open the envelope and looked at the message.

I looked up to my mother and she seemed terrified. She had her head turned away. 'All over?' she said.

'Not yet. But it look like nearly. They want us to come.'

'Oh.' She breathed out with relief. I, too, felt a little easier, for I had thought he was dead. He had been critical for sometime now and any news short of death news was relief of some sort. I said, 'We'll have to expect anything any time. No point in thinking he'll come back.'

'Oh, I know,' she said.

'You don't have to break down or anything if we hear the worst. I mean you realise what the position is?'

'I realise, but – I don't know.'

'Look, let's face up to things, eh. Let's try and see what we could do.'

I, myself, was still very ill. The dog-bites had given me a lot of ague and fever, and I had had about ten injections against blood-poisoning. I had been delirious for some while. To add to that I had had a heavy cold on account of the soaking I had taken. I had now got past the delirium stage, and also the worst of the cold was over, but I was still weak and shaky.

'One of us *must* go up,' I said. 'How you feel?'

She had been staring into space. She took in what I said.

'I was trying to work out something. This Freddie friend of yours, he seem to like you a lot. You think – '

'Better forget Freddie. We can't leave this sort of thing to strangers. In any case you think they'll let any stranger claim the body – if it so happens, you know.'

'Well, what you suggest? You tell me.'

I looked round at her. She seemed to be fighting away a storm of grief. She knew, as well as I did, that now was no time for

189

tears. There were things to be done. She, herself, had not been outside Mayaro in years. I could not honestly let her go into that wild, crazy Port-of-Spain. It would overwhelm her. Especially in this state of mind. I could not do it.

'*I'll go*,' I said.

'You mad or what? You could hardly walk, you talking about travelling to Port-of-Spain!'

'I'll go,' I said, 'tomorrow. I'll take three of those tablets and I'll go. Don't worry, because I'm not really feeling too weak now. I'll make it.'

'Look, don't forget what you just passed through. I have enough trouble already.'

'Watch!' I said. I rolled off from the bed and showed her I could stand up without swaying. I was really very dizzy but I did not tell her that. I made a few steps and I felt very doubtful as to whether I could travel tomorrow. 'You see?' I said, 'I'll be fine. I'll go up tomorrow. You could make the fare?'

'I'll have to see,' she said, 'things tight.'

'You mean you can't make the fare to Port-of-Spain and back?'

She was suddenly stung by this. 'Don't forget you in bed two weeks now. What you think – I picking up money on the ground?'

'All right. All right.'

'Look, I'll go down to the beach-house. I'll tell them, and they'll give me the little pay. Okay?'

'Okay, Ma.'

Her attitude had softened. She was looking down upon me. I had got back into bed and was lying on top of the sheets. I was very hot and my eyes were as though they were on fire.

She must have guessed this from my looks for she rested the back of her hand on my cheek.

'Good heavens!' she said.

'Don't worry.'

'You burning or something?'

'Don't worry, Ma. Get me some water and those tablets.'

When she came back with the water and the tablets and when I swallowed the tablets, she said, 'Gidharee called again this morning?'

'Yes.'

'You still think he really did that for spite?'

'I don't know what to think. I really don't know what to think?'

'I meself don't know what to think. Still, I'm glad I didn't go to the police station. Because you can't prove anything. But what puzzling me is, I mean to say, since that night when you come home delirious, and almost naked, I mean he come to see you every single day. So I can't see through that – you see what I mean. I mean he ain't vexed with you. Just the opposite, because he's so nice. Look, if it wasn't for that little money he give you I just don't know how we'd go through these little expense. You think that niceness genuine?'

'I don't know. All I know is what I tell you. I just seemed to revive and I was-soaking wet and nobody was there.'

'He said you left saying you was going home. Look, I can't understand this crazy thing. This man seem to like you a lot and I can't understand this. You think it have anything to do with the little girl? Because I think your father tell me you said you like her. Your father didn't happen to tell *him* anything about it? – I mean to make him vexed or anything?'

'Gidharee never mentioned anything about Rosalie,' I lied.

'I give up. I don't know what to say about this thing. Don't you ever go near those dogs again, that's all. And since you can't prove anything, and he so kind to you, we better try to forget it. Because, then, too, you say you can't remember nothing.'

191

'All right.'

There were so many times that I came to the edge of telling my mother the whole story of Rosalie, and so many times that I held back. Now was such a time. For I would have had to tell her about Boxing Night as well, and this I could not begin to do. Now, if it was my father, this would have been easy. I could have told him. Straight and frank. Also, talking of Mr Gidharee and the dogs, and what followed that afternoon with the dogs, would have been too much. She would have never understood.

The position was that I could not escape Mr Gidharee now. I knew it would not be beyond him to do what Ramdat talked about, because I had seen how cold-bloodedly cruel he could be. I could not have told my mother what had happened for with the distress of my father's illness already upon her, this would have finished her off. With her being away at work during the week, Mr Gidharee had come and we had talked privately and he had said he'd put his cards on the table. He had made it plain that I could not back-pedal on Rosalie. So there was only one choice left for me – short of fleeing Mayaro. And if I left Mayaro it would mean leaving my mother behind. I had come to make a deal with him and as far as I was concerned it was settled and sealed.

I lay thinking back on these last strange days. All through those moments of my delirium the four dogs of Mr Gidharee had haunted me, and Ma had thought I was going mad. Here, on the bed, in these fits, I had cried out at Rover and Lion, and had kicked out against Tiger, and once when I tried to fell Hitler I had fallen on my back onto the floor. The dogs had become that much alive in my mind and very often my screams had sent my mother running into the room. But in this present week, with Mr Gidharee being so friendly and suddenly generous to me, and with such kind promises, along with the money gift, the terror of that Cedar Grove day was beginning to fade.

My mother was still standing by the bed. I looked up weakly at her.

I said, 'That litttle girl – Rosa or Rosalie or something – you know she came to see me?'

'You mean his daughter? Oh yes?'

'Yes. She is a very nice girl.'

'She look so. She talk to me very nice.'

'Oh, you know her?'

'Oh yes. Every time she meet me now she does stop and talk.'

'She and Gidharee came to see me yesterday. I mean she was – she was really, really nice.'

Ma looked at me and there was a little smile on her face. 'Aha, so that's the way, eh? So what about Joan now?'

'I don't know.'

'You don't know?' She looked shocked to hear me say that.

'Joan is a nice girl – but, you know.'

'But this Gidharee girl fulling up your eyes now.'

'I don't know.' I tried to smile. I had to take this part as easily as I could and I had to be very smart.

She said: 'Well, listen boy, you sick and you don't know your own mind. Wait, and when you get better, you'll see.'

I was looking at her closely as she talked. The storm of my father's condition had really hit her hard, and I could see that although we were talking about Rosalie, she was all grief for him. To cheer her up I thought of telling her about the huge cocoa lands Mr Gidharee had bought in Cedar Grove – and which would be *ours* – but I would have had to explain, telling her of my decision on Rosalie, and why, and I could not face up to that.

'All right, Ma,' I said, 'leave me a little now. I think I'll sleep.'

'All right, and tomorrow you'll go?'

I was already sliding away into sleep when I heard her come back, sobbing, into the room.

'What's wrong?' I sat up.

I didn't want – I didn't want him to have a *pauper* burial,' she said, and burst into tears.

'What pauper burial! We bringing him home. Right here.'

'Where we'll get the money?' she stared at me, wide-eyed.

I held her hand. 'Ma, look, we can't talk now, but we'll talk.'

And realising that I could not keep my secret from her forever, and that she would have to know what was going on, and very soon, I said, 'Look, Ma, you see Mr Gidharee and me – we is good friends. Look, I have plenty to tell you but I don't know how to start. But let me sleep now – but don't worry about money because from now on we ain't hard up. No I ain't delirious now, I talking facts, so don't look at me so funny. But I must sleep a little now, okay? We have plenty to talk. When I get up I'll tell you everything.'

28

The next morning I left for Port-of-Spain. I did not go along the Manzanzilla Road, as I did not want to pass through Sangre Grande. I took the San Fernando route, through Rio Claro and Princes Town. This was another strange journey but I was not thinking of it much. I was thinking of my father.

Outside, the places were very shadowy in the early dawn and this made me feel even more desolate. Fears for my father kept crowding in upon me. And with them, memories of other days came to mind.

All the fine things we had done together – Pa and I – even

distant things from Down-the-Beach days, were with me now. Even the little things at Pierre Hill, such as sitting beside him on the settee and his putting his arm about my neck and being my chum as well as my father; all the numberless things which I could think of and feel so sharply without being able to tell of.

And yet, if this was goodbye to happy days, perhaps I should be grateful for having Mr Gidharee. Perhaps, grateful even for the dogs. *For I'd never be in want again.*

My father had worried himself about whether I would succeed in life, but now, with all that land on Cedar Grove, rich with fruit and rice and ground provisions, and with cocoa stretching far alongside the river, there could be nothing but success. I already knew a little about cocoa, and there was bound to be a big demand for fruit in Port-of-Spain. I thought of the great wastage on Mr Gidharee's land. This did not bother me before but it began to do so now. It was odd how trade and business had meant nothing to Mr Gidharee's generation. Only yesterday I was asking Mr Gidharee himself about cocoa prices and I was amazed to see what business could be done. After next month – after my engagement to Rosalie – when I would be helping to manage things, I would surprise him. There was a lot of planning in my head. Cedar Grove was now my goal in life.

I was jolted from my thoughts as the bus pulled into Rio Claro. I got out and caught the bus for Princes Town.

Settling myself again I began thinking of the new life ahead, and then, thinking back, Joan was big in my mind. I had given her up without any explanation and I had kept a silence in spite of her letters. It was a bitter decision but there was no other choice. The thing for me to do now was to forget. But I could not easily forget.

I was looking outside but seeing Joan's pleasant smile and fatty cheeks in my mind, and for some strange reason I was thinking of her just as she was at that Discovery Day fair, and I was remembering how I was dancing with her, holding her closely, and I felt intense pain inside.

I leaned against the seat in front of me, my face in my hands, and I was lost in the thought of Joan. When, after some time, I felt a touch on my shoulder and I looked up, the bus had arrived in Princes Town.

San Fernando came about half-an-hour later, and directly there was no more time for dreaming. After I had phoned the Colonial Hospital from there, as Mr Gidharee had asked me to do, as a precaution, I had to hasten to send him a telegram so he could start making arrangements for the funeral. Although I had been preparing for the worst, I was bewildered now and began sweating profusely. Through the haze of my thoughts I knew I had to get to Port-of-Spain as soon as possible. I rushed down to the railway station.

29

Today made it a week since Pa had gone to Paradise. No barking of dogs disturbed Pierre Hill as Mr Gidharee and I walked up the road. There were a few strays lying in the road and they barely raised their heads as we passed. It must have been as strange for them, as it was for me, that we should go by without the Tobago dogs, but I did not ask any questions.

'You ever cut bamboo before, Shell?'

'Not really.'

'So you never even make a tent?'

I laughed. 'Don't forget I never get engaged or married before.'

'No, I don't mean a tent for marrieding. Any tent. Like for a bazaar or anything.'

'Oh, I know what you mean. No, I never really build one.'

We walked a long way in silence until we got to Spring Flat. Here, it was calm and cool as always, with the immortelles shading out the sun, and with the quietness broken only by the chirruping of insects and by the birds in the trees.

'Mr Gid.'

'Yes?'

'Something I have to tell you.'

'Aha.' He looked at me.

'You know that thing – this ceremony business – I feeling a little scared.'

'Well, you don't look a *little* scared – you look scared like hell.' We both burst out laughing.

I said: 'Serious now, I mean I don't know about all this kind of thing. I mean the things to do, and so on. I don't know if I'll do it right.'

'You don't have to worry about that. Well show you everything. A Hindu engagement ain't nothing, boy.'

'Hope so.'

I felt very close to him and fond of him. I knew that if he said the engagement would go well it would go well. Thinking of the way he had treated us with my father's funeral, doing everything, and being so efficient and good, and spending his own money so freely, I felt nearly as close to him as I had felt to my father.

'You quiet all of a sudden, boy. You worried?'

'I was, but not now.'

'About what?'

'About this same ceremony business, but you say it ain't nothing.'

'Oh. How you like me gun. You ain't say nothing about me gun.'

'I was going to ask you about – ' I stopped.

'A gun is as good as those four buggers. You see it? Hold it.'

He took the gun off his shoulder and put it into my hands. It felt quite heavy and strange and it was the first time I had held a double-barrel gun. I would have liked to aim with it but it was cocked and I just passed my hand over the polished butt and gave it back to him.

'Nice gun,' he said. 'Boy, in the bush, if you have a gun and a cutlass you don't want nothing else.'

This made me want to ask about the dogs but I could not bring myself to do so. I did not want to think of what might have happened. We turned into Cedar Grove.

We walked in silence under the canopy of green and with the birds singing madly in the trees. We walked past our plantation and past our new piece of cocoa land and through the trees I could see Ortoire – brown and lazy – sliding along. I had never been this far into Cedar Grove and the place was very strange, with the forest looking denser and seeming to encroach upon the road. After about another half-a-mile, bamboo patches appeared on either hand.

Mr Gidharee rested his knapsack and his gun on the ground beside a bamboo clump and he pulled out his cutlass and stuck it into the ground. I pulled out mine and wiped the blade on the grass.

He said: 'You want to take a little rest before we start to cut?'

'No let's cut and go back out. We have a lot to do.'

He was taken aback. 'Like you want to build the tent today, boy. You anxious?'

'Aha.'

He seemed very moved. 'Don't worry. We have plenty time. But I like you spirit. Don't worry, everything will be okay.'

'I know,' I said.

'Everything will be okay, me old Shell,' he said.